by Sir Arthur Conan Doyle.

D0229661

For my grandchildren, as always, with love

THE CASE OF THE
RANJIPUR
RUBY

ANTHONY READ

Illustrated by
DAVID FRANKLAND

WALKER
BOOKS

First published 2006 by Walker Books Ltd
87 Vauxhall Walk, London SE11 5HJ

2 4 6 8 10 9 7 5 3 1

Text © 2006 Anthony Read
Illustrations © 2006 David Frankland

The right of Anthony Read and David Frankland to be identified as author and illustrator respectively of this work has been asserted by them in accordance with the Copyright, Designs and Patents Act 1988

This book has been typeset in Cochin

Printed and bound in Great Britain by J.H. Haynes & Co. Ltd

British Library Cataloguing in Publication Data:
a catalogue record for this book is available from the British Library

ISBN-13: 978-1-4063-0088-8
ISBN-10: 1-4063-0088-8

www.walkerbooks.co.uk

Contents

ONE

Wiggins climbed the rickety ladder with great care. It was old and wobbly and it creaked alarmingly as he ascended step by step, rung by rung, trying to keep his balance as he clung on with one hand. His other hand held a cord attached to one corner of a long canvas banner, whose weight kept pulling him sideways. When it flapped in the breeze, he almost lost his footing.

"Don't look down!" Beaver warned, holding onto the ladder for all he was worth.

"Don't look down?" Queenie echoed scornfully. "What you on about?"

"I heard that if you look down when you're high up, you get giddy and fall off."

"But he's only four steps up."

"Yeah, but … all the same … if he *was* higher

up, and he *was* to look down…"

"Oi!" Wiggins shouted. "Never mind all that. Just keep hold of the ladder and stop this thing blowing about."

"Oh, right. Sorry, Wiggins." Beaver grinned sheepishly and grabbed the banner.

Standing behind Beaver and Queenie, Sarge, a large man in a dark-blue uniform, watched Wiggins carefully. He pointed to the post on the corner of the ornate iron arch with his one good arm – his other sleeve was empty, folded back and held up with a safety pin. Wiggins clambered higher and started to tie the cord round the post.

"That's it," Sarge called. "Tie it round there. Nice and neat, now. We don't want no granny knots comin' undone and droppin' the banner on folks' heads, do we?"

"No, Sarge," Wiggins replied.

"Clove hitch and two half-hitches, like I showed you."

"Right, Sarge." Wiggins looped the cord in the simple knot that Sarge had taught him earlier, and pulled the end tight.

"There. How's that?"

"Good lad. Now the other end, and we'll be hunky-dory."

Sarge was a retired soldier who guarded the entrance to the Bazaar, a large arcade with a high glass roof, in a side road off Baker Street. He lived alone in a small lodge alongside the big iron entrance gates, with a door that opened in two halves, like a horse's stable door, so that he could look out over the lower half and keep an eye on anyone passing in or out. Or even simply passing by, which is how he'd got to know Wiggins and the rest of the gang of urchins who called themselves the Baker Street Boys (even though three of them were actually girls). They often helped him by running errands or doing little jobs that he found difficult with only one arm, when he would joke that they really were "lending a hand".

Wiggins finished tying up the other end of the banner and was just climbing down when a woman's voice rang out from inside the Bazaar.

"Sergeant! What's going on there?"

A small, dark-haired woman, almost as wide as she was tall, marched towards them, shaking a finger at Sarge.

"Who are these children and what are they doing with my banner?" she demanded, quivering indignantly and looking as though she was about to burst out of the scarlet satin dress that strained to contain her ample figure.

Sarge stood to attention and snapped his hand to his cap in a smart salute that made the row of medals on his chest clink and the three gold stripes on his arm gleam in the pale sunlight.

"These, madam?" he asked. "Why, bless you, they're me little helpers. Couldn't have managed it without 'em."

"Hmph!" she snorted. "Let's have a look at it then."

She stomped through the gates and turned to examine the banner, stretched tightly across the archway. THE JEWELS OF THE CROWN, it proclaimed in big red letters, and on the next line: MADAME DUPONT'S JUBILEE TABLEAUX. ADMISSION 1 SHILLING, CHILDREN HALF PRICE.

"Not bad," said Madame Dupont. "Not bad at all. And you put that up, did you?"

She eyed the three Boys, sizing them up. Wiggins copied Sarge, standing to attention and raising his hand to his black billycock hat in a salute.

"That's right, missus," he replied. "The Baker Street Boys at your service."

"Good." She turned back to Sarge. "Reliable, are they, the Baker Street Boys?"

"Trust 'em with me life, madam."

"And so would Mr Sherlock Holmes," Queenie told her.

"Mr Holmes the famous detective?"

"The same," said Wiggins, then dropped his voice conspiratorially. "We work for him sometimes, don't you know."

"I see. Carrying messages and such like, I s'pose?"

"Helpin' him solve crimes, more like," Queenie said.

"Well I never."

"It's true," Wiggins assured her with all the confidence of his fourteen years. "Only don't go telling nobody, will you? 'Cos sometimes we have to work in secret, like."

"Don't worry, dearie, I'm very good at keeping secrets." She just managed to hide a smile, then beckoned to the three youngsters. "Now come with me."

❊   ❊   ❊

For someone so plump, Madame Dupont moved very quickly, and the three Boys had to hurry to keep up with her as she bustled her way back through the Bazaar. For many years, the Baker Street Bazaar had been home to Madame Tussaud's waxworks, until they moved to their own new building half a mile away. The rooms they had occupied were now used for all sorts of exhibitions and shows. Madame Dupont's was the latest. Her real name was Mrs Bridges, and she had been born and bred in London, but she thought her name sounded better in French, like her more famous competitor. Her waxworks were not as grand, or as good, as Tussaud's, but they managed to attract quite a number of visitors – especially people from the country, who were more easily impressed than Londoners.

The rest of the Bazaar housed a row of small shops along one side, mainly selling hats and ribbons and buttons and fancy stuff. The other side was used as a carriage repository, where rich people stored their coaches and carriages – though not their horses, who lived with their coachmen in stables and mews behind the big houses. Wiggins, Beaver and Queenie trotted past the line of neatly parked carriages as they followed Madame Dupont to the entrance of her show.

"Come along, come along!" she called, pushing open the double doors. "Stay with me and don't touch anything!"

As they stepped inside the doors into a small hallway, Queenie let out a scream and dived behind Beaver and Wiggins. Glaring at them was a Red Indian brave, complete with feathered headdress, his face fierce with war paint, brandishing a stone axe in his raised hand. Queenie was scared stiff. Even the two lads stopped short, their mouths dropping open.

"Keep him off me!" Queenie cried.

"It's all right," Wiggins reassured her, recovering fast from the shock of facing a savage warrior. "He can't hurt you."

"Look – he ain't movin'," Beaver added. "He ain't real."

Madame Dupont cackled with laughter, delighted at the effect of her model.

"Course he ain't!" she crowed. "He's made of wax. Ain't you never seen waxworks afore?"

Queenie shook her head, still nervous. The Red

Indian seemed very real until you looked hard.

"Ooh, that's a good 'un, and no mistake," Madame Dupont chuckled. "Fair put the wind up you, didn't we!"

Queenie nodded.

"Good. That's what he's there for. To make people jump."

"Hey, if you was to put a clockwork motor inside him," Wiggins suggested, "you could make him move his arm and wave his chopper."

"His tomahawk," Madame Dupont corrected him. "That's what they call it."

"Yeah," Beaver joined in. "If he was to wave his tommyhawk, that'd really make people jump."

Queenie shuddered at the idea, but Madame Dupont nodded shrewdly.

"That's not a bad idea," she said, looking hard at Wiggins. "You're a bright lad, ain't you. I s'pose that's why Mr Holmes employs you."

"That's right." Wiggins grinned at her. "He knows a good thing when he sees it."

"And so do I," she continued, "which is why I'm going to employ you too. Come along now. No time to stand there gawping. There's work to be done."

She clapped her hands then marched briskly through the inner doors, waving at the three Boys to follow her. They did so, cautiously, fearful of fresh shocks, and found themselves in a very large room with a high ceiling and marble pillars. Gas-lit alcoves lined the walls. In each of them was a group of waxwork figures, dressed in exotic costumes from various parts of the Empire.

Two fierce Zulu warriors wearing leopard skins and brandishing spears and shields stood alongside a South African settler holding a nugget of gold in one hand and a sparkling diamond in the other. In the next alcove, a bearded Sikh in a silk turban held up another big diamond. Further along, two South Sea Islanders displayed a heap of pearls in a large flat shell, and other figures in colourful garments showed more precious stones: blue sapphires from Ceylon, green emeralds from Africa, milky opals from Australia, and so on.

The three Boys stared around them in amazement. Then Queenie let out a little cry and pointed to the other end of the gallery.

"Look!" she said. "Her Majesty!"

And indeed, there was Queen Victoria herself –

or rather a wax model of her, wearing a black lace dress with a bright blue sash over one shoulder and a tiny crown on her head. There was something a bit odd about the eyes – one was almost crossed – and the cheeks were just a bit too red, but it was certainly the Queen.

Standing before her, bowing from the waist, was an Indian prince, splendidly dressed in a long embroidered coat, tight silk trousers and gold slippers with curly pointed toes. On his head was an elaborate turban with a jewel at the front from which sprouted a spray of peacock feathers. Beside him knelt an Indian boy, also wearing silks and satins and a turban. The boy was holding up a velvet cushion on which rested an enormous red jewel, which the prince was obviously presenting to the Queen.

"Cor," said Queenie, gazing at the scene. "Ain't that lovely?"

"Thank you, dearie," Madame Dupont said. "I am proud of my latest tableau."

"Low what?" Beaver asked.

"Tableau," Queenie explained. "That's like a picture, ain't it?"

"Quite right, dear," Madame Dupont told her. "A picture that tells a story without words."

"And what story is this one telling?" Wiggins asked.

"Why, it's the Ranjipur Ruby, of course."

"What's the Ranjipur Ruby?"

"That is," Madame Dupont said, pointing at the jewel. "I thought you was a bright lad."

"He is," Beaver piped up loyally. "Everybody knows that."

"And you ain't heard of the Ranjipur Ruby? It's the most beautiful ruby ever known. It comes from India, and the Raja of Ranjipur is going to present it to the Queen next week, as a loyal tribute."

"Who's the Raja of whatsit?" Beaver asked.

"He's a sort of king," Madame Dupont replied.

"And Ranjipur's his kingdom?" asked Queenie.

"That's right. It's part of India."

"Cor," Beaver said, gazing in awe at the blood-red stone. "Ain't you scared somebody might pinch it? It must be worth a fortune."

Madame Dupont threw back her head and hooted with laughter.

"Why, bless you, dearie," she chuckled when she

had got her breath back, "it ain't real. No more than my waxworks is real people. It's just a bit of coloured glass."

Beaver turned as red as the pretend ruby.

"Right," he stammered. "But if it *was* real ... if they *was* all real jewels..."

"Then I'd be as rich as Her Majesty and I wouldn't be here with you lot!"

"Well, they look real enough, and no mistake," said Wiggins, trying to save Beaver's blushes.

"But whatever's that?" asked Queenie. She pointed to a fearsome female figure standing in the background behind the Raja. She had six arms, wild hair and a black face with three eyes – except that the third eye, which had been in the middle of the creature's forehead, was missing.

"That," said Madame Dupont, "is the heathen idol what the ruby was in. See the hole in the middle of her forehead?"

Queenie shuddered. Even though she knew it was only a wax model, the idol was still very scary.

"Come on," said Madame Dupont. "That's enough of that. This way."

She led them to a corner and pushed on what

looked like part of the panelling on a solid wall. To their surprise, it turned out to be a hidden door into a dark room filled with boxes and piles of odds and ends. Reaching inside, she pulled out a bulging canvas bag, which she handed to Beaver.

"Here," she said, "you look the strongest. You'd better carry it."

Beaver took the bag and looked inside. It was full of printed leaflets. Madame Dupont pulled one out to show them.

"These are the handbills advertising my new exhibition. I want you to go along the streets and give 'em out to everybody you see. I'll pay you sixpence apiece, all right?"

"How about a shilling each?" Wiggins asked with a grin.

"I knew you was a cheeky one, soon as I set eyes on you," Madame Dupont grinned back at him. "You can have half a crown for the three of you. All right?"

It took Wiggins barely a second to work out that a half-crown – two shillings and sixpence – meant ten pence each. His grin broadened.

"Done."

The bag full of leaflets was heavy even for Beaver, and after the three Boys had been handing them out in the street for half an hour or so his shoulder was starting to ache.

"This bag don't get no lighter," he puffed.

"How many has she put in there?" Queenie asked. "It's gonna take us all day to get rid of 'em."

"Why don't you have a rest for a minute, Beav?" Wiggins said. "Then we can start again in another street."

Beaver nodded gratefully and they turned off into a side street to find a good place to sit down. They were just settling into a sheltered doorway when they heard the sound of running feet. A moment later, a boy of about their own age raced past them. But this was no ordinary boy. This was one of Madame Dupont's waxworks come to life, an Indian boy dressed in silk and satin like a smaller version of the Raja presenting the ruby to the Queen. He was being chased by two fierce, dark-skinned men in long grey shirts, baggy pants and untidy cotton turbans. Their eyes glittered cruelly, and their faces were twisted in evil fury. One of them had a livid scar running from his eyebrow to his chin.

Looking around frantically for a way of escape, the boy turned into an alleyway. But his pursuers spotted him, and followed. Wiggins leapt to his feet.

"There's no way out of there!" he cried. "He's trapped."

"Come on, we gotta help him!" Queenie yelled.

They raced across the street and down the alley, Wiggins in the lead. Beaver, weighed down with the heavy bag, trailed in the rear. As they entered the alley, they saw the two men advancing on the boy, who was, as Wiggins had foretold, trapped in a corner of the courtyard at the end. One of the men grabbed the boy, while the other threw a twisted scarf round his neck, ready to strangle him.

"Leave him alone!" Wiggins shouted, leaping onto the first man's back.

The man swung round with a snarl of rage, trying to throw him off, but Queenie leapt at him too, kicking him hard on the shin. The second man turned angrily, and as he did so Beaver swung the heavy bag with all his strength, catching him on the side of the head and knocking him down. The first man was hopping with pain on one leg. When Wiggins gave him a shove he lost his balance and crashed to the ground on top of his partner. As he fell, Queenie took hold of the Indian boy's arm.

"Come on!" she called. "Run for it!"

And run they did – as fast as their legs would carry them.

Two

"Where to now?" Queenie gasped as the three chums and the Indian boy dashed out of the alleyway.

Beaver had dropped his heavy bag after biffing the man with it. For a moment he considered going back for it, but he quickly decided against.

"They'll be right after us," he said.

"HQ!" Wiggins ordered. "We'll be safe there."

"Come on," Queenie told the Indian boy, taking hold of his hand. "Stick with us."

"We'll look after you," Beaver added.

Glancing back over their shoulders every few seconds to make sure the men were not behind them, they ran flat out until they reached the safety of HQ. They tumbled down the steps into the secret cellar and pushed the door shut, puffing and panting as they tried to catch their breath.

Most of the other Boys were out, trying to earn pennies for food. Only Sparrow, the youngest and smallest of the gang, was at home as Wiggins, Beaver and Queenie burst in with the Indian boy in tow. Sparrow was standing in front of the stove, shuffling a pack of playing cards, trying to master a trick that he had seen a conjuror perform at the Imperial Music Hall, the theatre where he sometimes worked as a callboy. Startled by their sudden arrival, he lost his hold on the cards and they spilled from his hands, scattering all over the floor.

"Oooh," he groaned. "Look what you made me do!"

"Never mind that," Wiggins admonished him. "We got more important things to worry about."

Sparrow stared at the Indian boy.

"Cor," he exclaimed. "What show's he in? Ali Baba and the Forty Thieves? Aladdin and his Magic Lamp?"

"Less of your lip," Queenie scolded. "Can't you see he's Indian? And he's had a very nasty shock, so you better be nice to him."

"Oh. Sorry. Does he talk the lingo?"

The Indian boy was looking around the Boys'

hideaway in amazement, taking in the various bits and pieces with which it was furnished: the makeshift beds, the big table propped up with a block of wood, and Wiggins's special armchair. Now he smiled, and spoke for the first time.

"I say," he said, in perfect English, sounding like a lord, "what a spiffing place. Do you actually live here?"

The Boys stared at him, open-mouthed.

"Oh, forgive me," he continued. "I haven't thanked you chaps for rescuing me. I really am most awfully grateful."

"That's all right, old chap," said Wiggins. "Who was them geezers anyway?"

"Geezers?"

"Yeah, you know, blokes. Chaps. Men."

"Ah, geezers..." the boy rolled the word around his mouth, testing the sound of it. "Must remember that. Geezers..."

"Was they tryin' to rob you?" Beaver asked.

"I rather think they were trying to murder me."

Sparrow let out a whistle, and regarded him with more respect.

"Why?" asked Wiggins.

"Because of who I am, I suppose."

"Who are you, then?"

"Oh, I do beg your pardon. I haven't introduced myself. My name is Ravindranatharam."

"Crikey," said Sparrow, "that's a mouthful and no mistake."

"Yes I know, it is rather. You can call me Ravi."

"That's better."

"My father is the Raja of Ranjipur…"

"The ruby!" Wiggins and Queenie shouted together.

"You've heard of it?"

"Heard of it?" Wiggins said. "We was looking at it, this very afternoon."

Ravi looked shocked. "You mean it's been stolen?" he asked. "Oh my goodness! Do you know who took it?"

"Nobody took it," Wiggins told him. "No need to panic."

"We seen a copy of it," Beaver explained.

"In Madame Dupont's waxworks," Queenie said. "Come to think of it, there was two wax people there that was likely s'posed to be you and your dad."

"That's right!" Wiggins said. "Presenting the ruby to Her Majesty."

"You think that was really him?" Beaver asked, staring at Ravi with fresh interest. It was exciting to know someone who had actually had a waxwork made of them and put on public display.

Ravi looked puzzled. "But we haven't presented it yet," he said. "We have to wait for Queen Victoria to come back to London. I believe she's staying in her house on the Isle of Wight at the moment."

"That don't matter," Wiggins told him. Then he and Queenie explained about the waxworks exhibition, and the copies of all the precious stones that went into the crown jewels, and the places they came from.

"I say!" Ravi said when they had finished. "That sounds jolly interesting. Will you take me to see it?"

"Course we will, love," said Queenie.

"Now? We could go now?"

"Er, hang on a minute, Ravi," Wiggins chipped in. "Ain't you forgetting something?"

"What?"

"Them two blokes…"

"Ah, yes. The geezers."

"That's right. The geezers what was trying to murder you?"

"Yeah," Beaver joined in. "They're still out there."

"And like as not," added Queenie, "they still want to do you in."

Ravi smiled trustingly at them. "But I have you to protect me now," he said.

Beaver straightened his back, proudly. "That's it," he said. "You're with the Baker Street Boys."

"The Baker Street Boys?"

"That's us," Queenie said. She introduced herself and the others, and explained who they were and what they did. Ravi was fascinated.

"And you live here on your own, with no one to boss you about, looking after yourselves?" he asked.

"And lookin' after our friends," Beaver added. "You stick with us and you'll be all right."

"All the same," Wiggins cautioned, "you can't be too careful. Them two geezers looked like a couple of tough nuts. You got any idea who they were?"

"No idea at all."

Wiggins put on his deep-thinking expression, and stroked his chin as he had seen Mr Holmes do.

"They looked like they was from your country," he said.

"It's possible," Ravi replied. "There are some in Ranjipur who do not approve of my father giving away the ruby."

"How about you? What do you think?"

"Personally, I can't wait to get rid of the wretched thing. They say it carries a curse, you know."

The Boys stared at him in wonder. This could turn into a really exciting adventure. But Queenie had other thoughts.

"The ruby's got a curse on it," she said, "and you're givin' it to Her Majesty? Strikes me that ain't a very nice present."

Ravi shook his head. "The curse only applies to men who own the stone, not ladies."

"Oh, well, that's all right then," Wiggins grinned.

Ravi grinned back. "To tell you the truth, I believe my father can't wait to get rid of the ruddy thing, even though it's worth a king's ransom."

"Well, if Her Majesty don't want it, you can tell your dad to give it to me," Queenie joked. "I'd be all right with it!"

They all laughed, but stopped when Wiggins's sharp ears heard a sound from outside.

"Quiet!" he said, holding up one hand. "Somebody coming…"

They fell silent. Wiggins was right – they could hear footsteps on the stairs.

"More than one of 'em," whispered Sparrow.

They all held their breath, waiting nervously. The footsteps came nearer and stopped. The door burst open – and Shiner, Rosie and Gertie tumbled through it. They stopped at the sight of the others standing there.

"What's up with you lot?" Gertie demanded. "You look like you seen a ghost or somethin'."

"And who's 'e?" Shiner asked, pointing at Ravi. "What's he doin' 'ere and why's he all dolled up in fancy dress?"

Ravi glanced down at his opulent clothes, then at the Boys' scruffy rags.

"Yes," he laughed, "I suppose they do look rather fancy. I'm Ravi. How d'you do."

He stepped forward, took Shiner's hand and shook it, to the little boot-black's astonishment.

"Is 'e tryin' to be funny?" he asked, looking as

though he might punch Ravi on the nose.

Queenie quickly intervened. "Manners!" she admonished Shiner. "Ravi's a prince. Come all the way from India, to give Queen Victoria a precious jewel."

"Why?" Shiner wanted to know. "Ain't she got enough already?"

Queenie turned to Ravi with an apologetic smile. "This is my little brother, Albert. We call him Shiner, 'cos he shines shoes at Paddington Station. And this is Rosie, she sells flowers to ladies and gents."

Rosie smiled shyly and, because he was a prince, gave Ravi a little curtsy that made her blonde curls dance around her face.

"And this is Gertie..." Queenie continued.

"Gertie?" Ravi looked at the short ginger hair escaping from beneath Gertie's cap, and the ragged trousers ending just below her knees, and shook his head, puzzled. "I thought Gertie was a girl's name."

"She is a girl," said Queenie. "Though she don't like to admit it."

Gertie beamed, delighted at being mistaken for a boy.

"Ah, I see," said Ravi. "She is what one would call a tomboy."

"Anythin' a lad can do, Gertie can do."

"And better," Gertie said, with a broad grin.

"Well, I'm very pleased to meet you, Gertie." Ravi took her hand and shook it, heartily. "Are there any more of you?" he asked.

"No," said Queenie. "That's it. The gang's all here."

"Jolly good. What shall we do now?"

"Well," said Wiggins. "I s'pose the first thing we gotta do is get you back home safe and sound."

"Oh, do I have to? Can't I stay here with you? My tutor wants to send me to Eton College, and I really don't want to go to school."

"You got any money?" Shiner asked.

"Shiner!" Queenie rebuked him.

But the young prince was not offended. "I don't carry money with me," he replied.

"Nor do we," joked Sparrow. "We ain't got none!"

"We'd love for you to stay with us," Queenie told Ravi gently. "But it just wouldn't be right. 'Sides which, your folks'll be startin' to worry about you and wonderin' where you got to."

"Queenie's right," Wiggins said. "I dare say they'll be sending out search parties if you ain't back soon. So where're you staying?"

Ravi sighed in disappointment. "If I go, may I come back and see you all again?"

"Only if you don't tell nobody where this place is," Wiggins told him.

"This is HQ, and it's secret," Beaver added.

"I won't breathe a word. I promise."

"All right. Now, where are you living?"

"We're staying in Lord Holdhurst's house, on the corner of Baker Street and Dorset Street."

"That's not far. We'll come with you. Not you lot," he told the younger Boys. "It don't need all of us. Just Beaver and Queenie."

The other four Boys moaned at being left out, but Wiggins shook his head firmly.

"Be too much of a crowd," he told them. "We don't wanna draw attention to ourselves, not if Ravi here's in danger."

"Let's go then," said Queenie, taking Ravi's hand again. "Your dad'll be pleased to see you back."

"My papa's not there," Ravi replied. "He's taken

his guns to Scotland, with Lord Holdhurst."

"Are they gonna shoot somebody?" Rosie asked, looking worried.

Ravi laughed.

"Not somebody. Something. Deer and stags and birds. At home he shoots tigers."

"That's terrible," said Rosie. "Poor things."

"Not when they're man-eaters," Ravi replied. "Sometimes they attack villages and kill people and carry off their children."

"Oh! I'm glad we don't have man-eating tigers in this country."

"No," Queenie agreed. "In this country it's people what kills people. Come on, let's get goin'."

THREE

There was no sign of the two men as Wiggins,
Beaver and Queenie left HQ with Ravi. But the
Boys were taking no chances as they made their
way through the streets. Queenie walked a little
way ahead, acting as lookout. Wiggins and Beaver
kept Ravi between them and stayed close to the
buildings, nervous that at any moment the men
might leap out at them and try to murder them all.

Fortunately, there were plenty of people about as
they entered a busier street. The muffin man passed
them, balancing a tray of warm muffins on his head
and ringing his hand bell to attract customers –
a steady stream of maids and cooks came out to buy
his wares for tea. Further down the street, scullery
maids brought cutlery to a knife-grinder who
crouched over his barrow at the edge of the

pavement, creating showers of sparks like fireworks on Guy Fawkes night as he sharpened knives and scissors on his spinning grindstone.

"We should be all right now," Beaver said. "Too many people about for 'em to try anythin' here."

"All the same," Wiggins replied, "we can't be too careful. Keep your eyes open."

They reached Lord Holdhurst's house safely. Ravi climbed the steps to the front door and tugged at the brass bell pull. After a moment, the door was opened by a maid aged about sixteen, wearing a uniform of blue dress, white apron and frilly white cap.

"Oh, Prince Ravi!" she exclaimed. "Where've you been? Captain Nicholson's been going on something awful. He wants to see you at once. In the drawing room."

"Thank you, Annie," said Ravi. "And I want to see him. I want him to meet my new friends." He turned and beckoned to the three Boys. "Come on," he urged. "This way."

He bounded up the broad marble stairway leading from the imposing hall. The Boys hesitated, awed by the oil paintings and gilt mirrors and rich velvet drapes, then followed him. Annie watched them curiously, a little smile on her lips. As they passed her, she quickly reached out and plucked Wiggins's and Beaver's hats off their heads, gently shaking her head and tutting quietly.

In the drawing room at the head of the stairs, two men were waiting. One, a slim, handsome Englishman in his late thirties, smartly dressed in a long black jacket and pinstriped trousers, was leaning against the marble mantelpiece, stroking his fair moustache. He was standing on a large rug, made from the skin of a magnificent tiger, complete with head. Its jaws were open wide in a snarl that showed its fearsome fangs. At first sight it looked as though it were still alive. When Queenie saw it she shrank back nervously for the second time that day.

The other man in the room was older and fatter, an Indian wearing a dark grey coat, buttoned to the neck, and tight white trousers. Both men had stern expressions on their faces, but the Indian's was much more sour. His mouth was pinched tight, as though he had been drinking vinegar. He got to his feet as Ravi entered the room.

"Ravi!" the Englishman snapped. "Where have you been? I gave you strict instructions that you were not to leave this house without an escort. Anything could have happened to you."

"It very nearly did," Wiggins said as he followed Ravi into the room.

The man stared at him.

"What the—? Who are these ragamuffins? What are you doing with them?"

"These are my friends: Wiggins, Beaver and Queenie. They're the leaders of the Baker Street Boys."

"They are disreputable guttersnipes—"

"'Ere, hold on, guv'nor!" Wiggins protested. But the man continued without a pause.

"—and they have no place in a respectable house filled with valuable things. What on earth are you thinking of, bringing them in here?"

"The captain is indubitably correct," the other man added in a heavy Indian accent, wagging his finger angrily at Ravi. "Your father would by no means be giving his approval."

"My father is not here," Ravi replied calmly. "But if he were, I'm sure he'd be giving my chums a big thumbs-up. They saved my life, don't you know!"

"What tommyrot is this?" the captain asked.

"It ain't tommyrot, your honour," Queenie blurted out. "It's the God's honest truth. Ain't that right, lads?"

Wiggins and Beaver nodded earnestly.

"Cross my heart and hope to die!" said Beaver. "If it hadn't been for us, Ravi would've been a goner, and that's for sure."

"Oh my goodness!" the Indian man exclaimed. "An accident?"

"It wasn't no accident, guv'nor," said Wiggins. "It was 'tempted murder."

"Murder?! Oh my goodness, gracious me!"

"Now then, let's all keep calm, shall we?" the captain said. "Tell me exactly what happened. I'm Captain Nicholson by the way, Prince Ravindranatharam's tutor, and this gentleman is Mr Ram Das, the Raja's dewan."

"His what?" Wiggins asked.

"His dewan," Ravi said, carefully pronouncing it dee-wan. "It's like a prime minister. He runs things for my father."

The dewan inclined his head solemnly, and sat down. The captain sat down too, facing the four youngsters, and gestured to Ravi to begin.

"Well, it was like this," Ravi started. "I decided to do a little exploring – it gets awfully boring, you know, being cooped up in here, and you'd gone off somewhere—"

"Yes, yes, I had business to attend to. Get on with it, boy."

"I was in the street, and there were these two geezers…"

The captain's eyebrows shot almost to the top of his forehead.

"I beg your pardon?" he said sharply.

"You know – geezers. Fellows. Men," Ravi explained impatiently. Captain Nicholson covered his mouth with his hand and coughed – Wiggins was sure he was hiding a smile. Ravi continued, describing what had happened and how the Boys had come to his rescue. The two men listened with shocked faces. When Ravi had finished, the captain turned to the Boys.

"Well," he said, "it seems we owe you chaps an apology. And a vote of thanks."

"We was only doing our duty, Captain," Wiggins said. "It's our business, you know, fighting crime."

"Is it, indeed? Well done, anyway. Tell me, these

men – these, er, geezers. Did they have knives? Cudgels? What?"

"No," Wiggins told him. "They was trying to strangle him."

"With a sort of scarf, like a neckerchief," Queenie added.

The dewan leapt to his feet in alarm.

"No!" he exclaimed. "It's not possible! Not here."

The others stared at him, surprised by his look of fear.

"What isn't?" the captain asked.

"The stranglers. The Thugs. They were all destroyed fifty years ago. How can they be here, now, in London?"

The dewan was so agitated that Captain Nicholson had to ring for some tea to help him calm down. Supervised by the butler, Mr Hobson, Annie brought in a large tray laden with fine china cups and saucers, a silver teapot and a milk jug. Another maid brought a tray of plates filled with little cakes and tarts, which the Boys eyed hungrily. While the dewan was drinking his reviving cup of tea, Annie served Wiggins, Queenie and Beaver.

Mr Hobson, an imposing figure with a shiny bald head and a striped waistcoat, regarded the Boys with great disdain, but Annie smiled at them and gave them a wink when he wasn't looking. They were all terrified that they would break the delicate cups, and were not sure if they liked the tea, which tasted odd and scented, though it was all right with lots and lots of sugar. But they very quickly disposed of the cakes, each of which made only a single sweet mouthful to the ravenous youngsters.

By the time the Boys had polished off all the cakes, the dewan had recovered enough to talk about the stranglers.

"For hundreds of years," he explained, "there was a secret cult in India called Thuggee. Its members were known as Thugs. They worshipped Kali, the goddess of destruction. They used to join up with travellers on the road and make friends with them until they reached a good spot, far from anywhere. Then they would fall on the unsuspecting people and kill them."

"What'd they want to do that for?" Beaver asked.

"To rob 'em, I 'spect," said Queenie.

"Yes, they did rob them," the dewan went on.

"But they killed them as a sacrifice to Kali. The goddess did not allow them to shed blood, so they would strangle their victims, with a handkerchief."

Wiggins let out a whistle. "Just like them two tried to do to Ravi!" he said.

"That is correct," the dewan replied.

"Ah yes, I remember hearing something about all that," said Captain Nicholson. "But it was all finished fifty or sixty years ago, surely?"

"It was," the dewan confirmed. "It was eliminated by your people and there have been no killings since then."

"So why should they start up again now? And here in London?" the captain asked.

"And why should they want to kill Ravi?" added Wiggins.

"Revenge," said the dewan, looking very serious.

"Revenge? What for?"

"The ruby," the dewan replied. "The Raja's father took it from an idol of the goddess."

"That horrible thing with six arms and a black face and a red tongue stickin' out!" Queenie cried.

"That sounds like a fair description of Kali," the

captain agreed, looking surprised. "How did you know that?"

"Madame Dupont's got a model of it in her wax-work show," Wiggins said.

"Really? Where's that?"

"Right next door, in the Baker Street Bazaar. We seen it this very afternoon."

"Good heavens! Fancy that."

"Can we go and see it?" Ravi asked keenly.

"*May* we go and see it," the captain corrected automatically. "No you may not. I think under the circumstances it would be unwise for you to go anywhere near it, or even to leave this house until this business is sorted out."

"But I have my friends to look after me now."

"You were lucky once. You may not be so fortunate a second time."

Ravi groaned and pulled a face.

"Stop this foolishness at once!" the dewan snapped angrily. "And remember who you are."

"The dewan is quite right," the captain said, getting to his feet. "Now say goodbye to your friends. I think it's time they left."

The three Boys stood up, reluctantly. What they

had heard was all very exciting, and they did not want to miss anything. Plus there was always the chance that, if they stayed, Annie might bring in more cakes and even sandwiches or muffins.

"Ain't you gonna send for the coppers?" Wiggins asked.

"What is coppers?" the dewan asked, looking puzzled. "Are they asking for money? Small coins?"

"No, sir," the captain told him. "Copper is a common word for a policeman."

"'Cos if you are," Wiggins went on, "Inspector Lestrade's your man. We know him well."

"That's right," said Beaver. "We've solved lots of cases for him."

"We are not wishing for police," the dewan said sharply.

"Don't blame you," Wiggins told him. "You'd be better off with Mr Holmes."

"Mr Sherlock Holmes? The famous detective?" the captain asked.

"That's right, sir."

"I suppose you've solved lots of cases for him, too?"

"Yes, sir. His house is only just up the street.

He could be here in a few minutes."

The captain clearly did not believe Wiggins but gave him a friendly smile all the same, looking amused. The dewan, on the other hand, glared at them angrily.

"What is all this nonsense?" he demanded. "We do not wish for police or detectives. Kindly remove yourselves from this house immediately!"

The captain gave a little shrug, and turned to Annie, who had been standing quietly to one side.

"Show our young visitors out, if you please," he instructed her.

Annie moved towards the door, but before she got to it there was a commotion outside and a large Indian gentleman in a loud tweed suit rushed into the room. His huge curly moustache wobbled as he advanced towards Ravi, shaking his head sadly, his arms outstretched.

"Oh, Ravi," he cried. "Ravindranatharam, my poor, poor, boy!"

"Uncle Sanjay," Ravi said. "What is it?"

"Dreadful news… I bring truly dreadful news." He took Ravi's two hands in his, and looked into his eyes. "Your dear father. My dear brother. Dead…"

Ravi said nothing. He was too shocked to speak. Captain Nicholson hurried to comfort him. "How?" he asked Uncle Sanjay. "What happened?"

"An accident. While he was out fishing. He drowned."

"When?"

"His body was discovered in the loch last night. Lord Holdhurst is taking care of everything up there. I caught the first train to London to bring the sad tidings."

Ravi closed his eyes and gripped his uncle's hands tightly. The captain leant over and put one hand on his shoulder, squeezing it in silent sympathy.

The dewan raised both hands to heaven and let out a piercing wail.

"Aieeeee!" he cried. "It is the curse! The curse of the Ranjipur Ruby!"

FOUR

The four younger Boys listened with open mouths and wide eyes as Wiggins told them about the Thugs and the curse on the Ranjipur Ruby.

"Oh, poor Ravi," Rosie said sadly. "Losin' his dad like that."

Everyone nodded sympathetically. Then Queenie suddenly clapped a hand to her mouth.

"Oh, my word!" she said. "It ain't half 'poor Ravi'."

"What d'you mean?" asked Wiggins.

"Well, if his dad was the Raja of Ranjipur, and he's dead now, that makes Ravi the Raja, don't it?"

"Yeah, I s'pose it does."

"And if he's the Raja…"

"Oh, crikey … that means he owns the ruby!"

"Oh, Lor'. What we gonna do?" Beaver asked.

"Ain't much we *can* do, is there?" Wiggins said. 'Less we can find a way to get the curse lifted."

They all sat round the big table in HQ, feeling gloomy and helpless. Suddenly Beaver straightened up, looking worried.

"Oh dear," he said. "I just remembered somethin'."

"What?" asked Wiggins.

"Madame Dupont's bag of leaflets... It's still in that alley."

"Best place for it, I 'spect," said Shiner.

"Shiner!" Queenie reprimanded him. "She paid us money to hand out them leaflets."

"How's she gonna know if you ain't?" asked Shiner, unabashed.

"Queenie's right," said Wiggins. "We gotta go back and finish the job."

"Why don't we all go?" Sparrow suggested. "If we all help to hand 'em out, we'll get the job done quicker, right?"

They approached the alleyway nervously, especially as it was beginning to get dark. Queenie told them, "There's safety in numbers – nobody's gonna hurt us if we're together." But they were still relieved to find no sign of the men in the alley or in the little courtyard at the end. There was no sign, either, of the bag or the leaflets. In fact, the only thing they found was a small bag made out of stiff blue paper, half full of brownish white crystals that turned out to be sugar. Wiggins grinned and slipped it into his pocket, happy that they would be able to sweeten their bedtime cocoa that night.

"Now what we gonna do?" asked Beaver.

"Only one thing we *can* do," Queenie replied. "Own up."

Disconsolately, they trooped off to the Bazaar, where they were stopped at the gate by a cross-looking Sarge.

"Halt!" he shouted as they tried to slip past him. "Line up there! A nice straight line now... That's it."

They stood stiff and still like soldiers on parade while he walked along the line, glaring fiercely at them.

"Madam wants a word with you lot," he said. "And so do I. I spoke up for you. Told madam you could be relied on. And what d'you do? You let me down."

"But Sarge," Wiggins pleaded. "We can explain..."

"Quiet! Did I say you could speak?"

"No, Sarge, but—"

"Save it for madam. Atten-shun! Left turn! Quick march!"

And he marched them off through the Bazaar towards Madame Dupont's gallery, to the amusement of shoppers and visitors and a coachman who was busy polishing one of the parked carriages. Madame Dupont was sitting in her ticket booth just inside the doors when they entered, but she quickly came out as Sarge ordered them to halt.

"What's all this?" she asked, staring at the line of seven Boys. "How many more of you are there?"

"This is all of us," Wiggins told her.

"Thank goodness for that," she said. "Right. It's you I want to talk to."

Reaching back into the booth, she dragged out the bag of leaflets, then stood facing the Boys with her hands on her hips.

"A young chap brought this in," she said. "Found it in Clarke's Court. Did you really think you could get away with dumping it instead of handing the leaflets out, like I paid you to do?"

"But we didn't dump it," Wiggins told her.

"Then what was it doing in Clarke's Court?"

"We dropped it there, 'cos we had to run for our lives," Queenie said.

"And when we went back for it, it was gone," Beaver added. "That's why we're here. We come to tell you."

"Run for your lives? What are you on about?"

"There was these two Indian Thugs," Beaver began to explain, his words tumbling out in a rush, "and they was trying to murder Prince Ravi, the one what's in your waxworks, only he ain't the prince no more, he's the Raja now his dad's dead, but we rescued him and then we had to run for it, or they'd have tried to murder us as well, and it's all because of the curse, you see, and the goddess of destruction and everythin', and…"

"Whoa! Whoa!" cried Madame Dupont, utterly confused and holding up both her hands. "I can't make head nor tail of what you're saying. What sort of cock-and-bull story is this?"

"It ain't a cock-and-bull story," Wiggins protested indignantly. "It's all real. Only Beaver here, he don't say much as a rule, but when he does, he sometimes gets a bit carried away, like…"

"Yes, yes. So why don't *you* tell me what happened?"

"Right. Sorry, Beav."

Beaver shrugged amiably. Wiggins took a deep breath and told her the whole story. When he had finished, she shook her head in disbelief.

"Still sounds like a fairy tale to me," she said, and turned to Sarge. "You served in India, didn't you, Sergeant?"

"I did, madam. That's where I lost this." He patted his empty sleeve. "To a Jezail bullet. Up on the North-West Frontier it was, fighting the Afghan rebels. We was advancing up a defile not far from the Khyber Pass..."

"Yes, yes," she said quickly, sensing that he was about to spin a long soldier's tale. "But did you ever hear about these Thugs – these, er, stranglers?"

"Well, madam, there's all sorts of bandits in India – dacoits they call 'em – but I never heard tell of that particular sort."

"The dewan said—"

"The dee who?"

"The dewan. He's a sort of prime minister."

Madame Dupont shook her head in exasperation.

"Princes and prime ministers and curses and stranglers. It gets worse and worse," she muttered. "Well, go on. What did he say?"

"He said they was all s'posed to have been wiped out fifty or sixty years ago," Wiggins told her.

"Oh well, that'd explain why I never heard of 'em," Sarge said. "Before me time."

Madame Dupont still did not look convinced.

"Where's this prince, this Ravvy, now?" she wanted to know.

"We took him back to his house," Wiggins told her. "Well, not *his* house, exac'ly, it's Lord Holdhurst's house, what he's staying in till they give the ruby to Her Majesty."

Madame looked relieved. "At last," she cried. "Lord Holdhurst – a real person! He is real, ain't he, Sergeant?"

"Lord Holdhurst, madam? I should say so. As a matter of fact, he used to own this Bazaar. His old man built it, you know. A real character, he was. They say he used to pop up from nowhere, so he could keep an eye on everything that was going on in here. He just used to appear, all of a sudden. Liked to give everybody a shock."

"How did he manage that?"

"Search me, madam. There was talk of underground tunnels and the like, but who knows? Mind, his house is only just over the back there."

"That's right," said Beaver. "See, if you was to go out of the Bazaar and turn left, then turn left again at the next corner and walk up Baker Street till you get to the next corner after that and then—"

Madame Dupont cut him short. "Never mind all that," she said. "Did you say the Raja of Ranjipur's dead? When did this happen?"

"Yesterday," said Wiggins. "In Scotland."

"Drownded," Queenie added. "While he was fishin'."

"What did he want to go and drown his self for?" Madame Dupont demanded peevishly. "Very thoughtless, that is. Ruined my best tableau. How can I show him presenting the ruby to the Queen if he's dead?"

"I don't suppose he could help it," said Beaver.

"It was the curse," said Queenie.

"The curse of the Ranjipur Ruby strikes again," Wiggins declared in his deepest voice.

Madame Dupont stared at him for a moment, as

if he were mad. Then suddenly her face cleared and her eyes sparkled with excitement.

"That's it!" she shouted. "Brilliant! I could kiss you, lad!"

Wiggins backed away nervously, wondering what on earth he had done to deserve such an awful threat.

"The public'll pay good money to see a ruby that's got a curse on it!" She rubbed her hands together in delight. "I'll talk to the newspapers – they'll love a story like that. Never mind about them leaflets. I'll have some new ones printed. Come back tomorrow and we'll have 'em on the streets while the news is fresh."

She dismissed the Boys and they trooped out of the gallery, heading for HQ and supper. With two shillings and sixpence in Queenie's pocket, they would be able to afford a hot baked potato each from old Ant's barrow, and still have money to spare for stale loaves from the baker's and leftover bits from the grocer's.

As they trailed back through the Bazaar, they were cheered up by the thought that they would not have to go to bed hungry. In high spirits, Gertie climbed up on one of the carriages parked along the side wall.

"Your carriage awaits," she joked. "Climb aboard, and I'll drive you all back home in style!"

The others started laughing, until Rosie suddenly pointed to the door of the next carriage. With a look of shock on her face, she cried out, "Look! Look there!"

Painted on the door was a familiar monogram. A curly letter "M".

"Oh, my oath," breathed Wiggins. "Moriarty!"

The Boys sat up late in HQ, talking about Moriarty. Could he have been involved in the attack on Ravi? Or even the death of Ravi's father? Was it only by chance that he was around the Bazaar now? Or was he plotting something – like stealing the ruby? After all, how could London's master criminal resist the temptation of such a rich prize?

Having no answers to these questions, the Boys agreed that there was only one thing to do: they must ask Mr Holmes. In any case, the great detective would want to know that his hated enemy was on the prowl again. And so next morning, while the streets were still wreathed in early mist and fog, they made their way to Number 221b and tugged at the brass bell pull. As usual, Billy opened the shiny black front door. And as usual, he tried to look down his snub nose at them.

"Oh, it's you lot," he grunted.

"Wotcher, Billy, me old mate," Wiggins replied cheerfully, knowing that this familiar greeting always offended the pageboy. "Kindly inform Mr Holmes that his Irregulars have got something of importance to report to him."

"Can't," Billy replied smugly. "He ain't here. Good day."

He tried to close the door on them, but Wiggins was too quick for him, and managed to jam his foot in the opening.

"In that case, we'll see Dr Watson. If he ain't gone with him."

"No," said Billy reluctantly. "He ain't. Er, hasn't."

"Jolly good," Wiggins grinned, putting on a posh voice. "Be a good chap and show us up, will you, old bean?"

Billy glowered at the Boys on the doorstep.

"Just you and you," he said, pointing at Wiggins

and Beaver. "Mrs Hudson wouldn't want the rest of you trampling her stair carpet."

Dr Watson was still wearing his dressing gown and slippers and finishing his breakfast when the two Boys were shown in. He greeted them with his usual warm kindness.

"I'm afraid Mr Holmes isn't here," he apologized. "He's been called away suddenly to investigate a mysterious death in Scotland."

Wiggins and Beaver looked at each other apprehensively.

"That wouldn't be the Raja of Ranjipur, would it?" Wiggins asked.

"Good heavens, how do you know that?" asked Dr Watson, greatly surprised.

"Well, that's sort of why we're here. That and the Thugs and Professor Moriarty."

"Moriarty! How on earth is he involved?"

"Well," said Wiggins, "it's like this…" And he proceeded to tell the doctor all that had happened. Dr Watson listened with great interest. When Wiggins had finished, he scratched his head and sat thinking hard.

"I wish Mr Holmes were here," he said. "I'm sure

he'd be able to make something of it, but I'm blessed if I can."

"Was you ever in India?" Wiggins asked.

"Indeed I was. I have a couple of bullet scars to remind me of it. I served as an army surgeon in the Afghan war."

"And d'you know anything 'bout the Thugs?"

"I've heard of them, of course. Who hasn't? But all that was over and done with years ago."

He got up, crossed to the other side of the room, selected a large book from the shelves on the wall and began thumbing through it.

"Ah, yes, here we are," he said, and began reading aloud. "The Thugs were a well-organized secret society of professional assassins who travelled in various disguises throughout India. They were suppressed by the government in 1840 thanks to the efforts of a British official, William Sleeman ... hmm, hmm ... strangled their victim by throwing a handkerchief or noose around his neck ... plundered then buried him ... all done according to ancient religious rituals including the sacrifice of sugar to their goddess, Kali..."

Wiggins dipped his hand into his pocket and

pulled out the blue paper bag. "Look what I found in the alleyway!" he said.

Dr Watson took the bag, opened it and nodded solemnly.

"Sugar! If these fellows aren't Thugs," he said, "they're giving a jolly good imitation. I'd say your friend Ravi is in grave danger."

FIVE

Inspector Lestrade regarded the paper bag with great suspicion. He sniffed at its contents, then licked one forefinger, dipped it into the bag and dabbed it carefully on his tongue.

"Sugar," he pronounced.

"Exac'ly," Wiggins agreed.

"Common-or-garden sugar," the inspector went on, leaning back in his office chair. "Nothing illegal in a bag of sugar. I've got several in my pantry at home."

"But yours ain't a sacrifice to the goddess Kali, is it?"

"No, it's to sweeten my tea, and put on my porridge and in Mrs Lestrade's puddings and pastries. That's what sugar's for."

"Not if you're a Thug and you're gonna murder

somebody in the name of Kali," Wiggins said.

Beaver and Queenie, who had accompanied Wiggins and Dr Watson to Scotland Yard, nodded vigorously. Inspector Lestrade looked puzzled.

"We've got plenty of thugs in London," he said. "I lock some of them up every day. But they don't go around with bags of sugar in their pockets – not unless they've stolen them."

"These ain't that sort of thug," Queenie said. "These are Indian Thugs."

"What is she on about?" Lestrade asked, irritated.

"Thugs in India are, or were, ritual murderers. They were followers of a secret cult called Thuggee," Dr Watson explained. "That's where our word for a ruffian comes from."

"Does it, indeed? And you're trying to tell me they're starting up over here?"

"Not exac'ly, no," said Wiggins.

"So what 'exactly' *are* you trying to tell me?"

"That somebody's trying to murder Ravi, and steal the Ranjipur Ruby."

"Who is?"

"Professor Moriarty."

Lestrade let out a long sigh.

"Oh, no," he groaned. "Not him again. How do you know?"

"We saw his carriage, in the Baker Street Bazaar," said Beaver.

"And?" Lestrade looked at him expectantly. "What was the phantom professor doing this time?"

"Er ... nothin'."

"He wasn't there," Queenie said.

Lestrade sighed again. "He never is."

"No, but his carriage was," said Wiggins.

"Nothing illegal about parking a carriage in the Bazaar," Lestrade said wearily.

"But he's up to something," Wiggins said. "He's gotta be. I know he is."

Lestrade got to his feet.

"You don't know, lad. You only think you do. Haven't you learned anything from Mr Holmes? Now get off out of here and stop wasting my time."

"I say, steady on, Inspector," Dr Watson intervened. "The Boys are only doing their duty as good citizens and reporting suspicious circumstances."

"Thank you, Doctor. But I'm a very busy man with lots of crimes to investigate. And all they've brought me is a bag of sugar, an empty carriage going nowhere, and some tale about an Indian lad being set upon in the street by two roughs – who were probably trying to rob him but got away with nothing, so no harm done."

"Well, if you put it like that, Inspector…"

"I do. Now if you don't mind, I have work to do. Good day to you."

The Boys were upset that Inspector Lestrade would not take them seriously. As they left Scotland Yard, Wiggins kicked the door frame in a temper.

"Why won't he listen to us?" he demanded.

"He thinks we're makin' it all up!" said Queenie. "Ain't that right, Doctor?"

"Perhaps he does," Dr Watson replied. "After all, we didn't present him with any real evidence, did we?"

"*You* don't think that, do you, Doctor?" Wiggins asked.

"No, no, of course not," the doctor replied quickly. But he didn't sound very convinced.

"Tell you what," Wiggins said. "Why don't you come with us and we'll show you Moriarty's carriage?"

The doctor hailed a cab and they all piled in for the journey back to Baker Street. As it stopped outside the Bazaar, Sarge hurried to open the door. He stepped back in amazement as Wiggins climbed out, followed by Queenie and Beaver.

"What's all this, then? Come into money, have you?" he asked, then raised his hand in a salute as Dr Watson emerged. "Oh, beg pardon, sir. I didn't see they was with you."

Dr Watson nodded, then looked harder at the commissionaire. Sarge stared back at him, a smile of recognition spreading across his face.

"Captain Watson?" Sarge asked. "Is it really you, sir?"

"Well, I never," said the doctor. "Sergeant Scroggs!"

"*Captain* Watson?" said Queenie.

"Do you know each other?" asked Wiggins.

"I should say we do," said the doctor. "This brave fellow saved my life when I got my first wound on the Khyber."

"And the captain saved mine when I was hit. Even if he did have to cut me arm off to do it."

"Yes, sorry about that," said the doctor. "But

there was no other way. Good to see you again, Sergeant. How are you keeping?"

"Well enough, thank you, sir. May I ask what you're doing with these young scamps?"

"Dr Watson's a friend of Mr Sherlock Holmes," said Wiggins.

"He helps him and all," added Queenie.

"Just like we does," Beaver said. "We've just come from Scotland Yard."

Sarge looked suitably impressed.

"Have you now?" he asked. "And what brings you back here?"

"We got something to show the doctor. This way, guv'nor."

Wiggins led the way through the Bazaar to the parked carriages.

"Just over here... Oh!"

Moriarty's carriage was no longer there. Where it had stood the night before there was now a smart coach, painted a shiny dark red. The Boys stared at it in dismay.

"It was right there! Honest," said Wiggins.

"Yeah, right there," Beaver confirmed.

They described the black carriage to Sarge. But

he didn't know anything about it, and couldn't say how it had got out of the Bazaar since last night.

"Don't see how it could have left without me seeing it," he said. "That's if it was here at all."

"It was, it was!" Beaver protested.

"We all seen it last night," Wiggins said, shocked that their friend could doubt them.

"In the dark, was it?" Sarge asked.

"It was getting dark, yeah," Wiggins answered. "But not so dark that we couldn't see the letter 'M' painted on the door."

"That's M for Moriarty," Queenie explained.

But Sarge knew nothing about Moriarty, which was not surprising – the master criminal always did everything in the deepest secrecy. In any case, Sarge explained, he hardly ever saw the owners of the carriages, only the coachmen who drove them.

"We seem to have drawn a blank," Dr Watson told the Boys. "I fear there is nothing more we can do for the moment, so I must leave you. I have patients to visit."

"Why won't nobody believe us?" Beaver complained when they were back in HQ and telling the others what had happened. The four younger Boys had stayed behind while Wiggins, Queenie and Beaver had gone to Scotland Yard with Dr Watson.

"If you'd took me with you, I'd've made old Lestrade and the doctor believe us," Shiner grumbled. He was cross at missing out on a ride in a cab and a visit to Scotland Yard.

"No you wouldn't," said Queenie. "You'd only have made it worse."

"Trouble is," Wiggins said, ignoring them, "Lestrade was right – I was forgetting what Mr Holmes taught me. We don't *know* nothing. We only *think* we know."

"We know what them Thugs tried to do to Ravi," said Beaver.

"That's right," Queenie agreed. "We seen 'em trying to murder him."

"No we didn't," Wiggins said. "We only *think* they was trying to murder him. They might have been trying to kidnap him."

"Why would they want to do that?" Sparrow asked.

"To hold him for ransom!" Rosie cried.

"Exac'ly," said Wiggins. "Well done, Rosie."

"What's ransom?" asked Gertie.

"It's when you take somebody prisoner, and say you'll only let him go if his people give you a lot of money," Queenie explained.

"Or something very valuable..." said Wiggins.

"Like the Ranjipur Ruby!" Sparrow exclaimed.

"Exac'ly. If Professor Moriarty is after it, he could have sent them two Thugs to capture Ravi and hold him to ransom for it."

The rest of the Boys gazed at Wiggins in admiration. Once again, he had proved how clever he was.

"Mind," he cautioned them, "we don't know that, neither. They could still have been trying to kill him. Out of revenge."

"What we gonna do, then?" Queenie asked.

"I dunno," Wiggins admitted. "But I'll think of something. First of all, we gotta warn Ravi. You young 'uns stop here. Queenie and Beav, come with me."

"If the police don't believe you, why should we?" Captain Nicholson asked.

He was standing with his back to the fireplace in

the drawing room of Lord Holdhurst's house, one foot resting casually on the tiger's head. A wisp of blue smoke curled round his face from the thin cigar between his fingers. He raised a quizzical eyebrow at the three Boys, who were standing in a row facing him, like schoolchildren who had been hauled up in front of the headmaster.

"'Cos we're tellin' the truth," blurted out Beaver. "Honest."

"They've already saved my life once," Ravi spoke up. "So I shall listen to what they have to say."

He was sitting on a long sofa next to his Uncle Sanjay, whose enormous moustache bounced up and down on either side of his chubby face as he nodded his head.

"I am being in complete agreement with Ravi," he said.

The dewan, who was sitting slightly apart from the others, gave a scornful snort.

"As you wish," he said. "Kindly proceed."

Wiggins took hold of the lapels of his ragged coat, as he had sometimes seen Mr Holmes do. "Like I say, we can't prove nothing – leastwise, not yet. But if Moriarty's about, you'd best watch out.

'Cos you can bet he's up to no good."

"Who is this Moriarty?" the dewan asked. "Is he some kind of badmash?"

"I dunno. What's a badmash?"

"A bad man," said the captain. "What we'd call a villain, or a crook."

"Oh yeah," said Wiggins. "He's the biggest badmash in London."

"Mr Holmes calls him the Napoleon of Crime," Beaver chipped in.

"Says he's got a finger in everythin' wicked in this city," Queenie added with relish.

The dewan snorted again, even more scornfully. "Then why is he not in prison?" he demanded.

"'Cos he's slippery as a serpent," said Wiggins. "And twice as cunning. He ain't a professor for nothing."

"I take it you've had dealings with him before?" the captain asked.

"Once or twice, guv'nor. One time he nearly did for Mr Holmes his self, not to mention Her Majesty Queen Victoria. And would have done, if it hadn't been for us. Only we're not allowed to talk about that, you understand."

"I see. It would seem that we're lucky to have you on our side."

"It would seem to *me*," the dewan sneered, "that you are having a very strong imagination, young man."

"Well, sir, if you means I can imagine what might happen if things go wrong, then p'raps I have. You need one if you're a detective."

The captain's mouth twitched in a small smile under his moustache. Ravi grinned openly. The dewan scowled, his face dark as thunderclouds.

"And do you imagine that this Moriarty is a follower of Kali?" he asked derisively. "Practising the cult of Thuggee to murder Prince Ravi?"

"I wouldn't put nothing past him," Wiggins replied. "I hope you've got that ruby somewhere safe."

"It is locked away. And only I have the key," said the dewan. He reached under his shirt and pulled out a large key hanging on a cord around his neck. "You see? It is never leaving my person."

"Good show," said the captain. "Can't say better than that, eh?"

Ravi grinned mischievously. "I'd say that having

that round your neck would be jolly handy for anybody wanting to strangle you," he teased.

The dewan was not amused. In fact, he turned so pale that Wiggins thought he was going to faint. But Ravi had not noticed. "I say," he chuckled, "I've had a rather jolly thought. If this geezer Moriarty wants to steal the ruby so badly, why don't we let him? Then he'll bring the curse down on himself, and that'll be him done for."

The dewan's face changed from pale to purple, and he looked as though he was about to burst. The captain stepped in quickly. "Ravi!" he snapped. "That is not funny. How can you joke about the curse at a time like this?"

"Sorry, Ram Das," Ravi apologized – although he did not look very contrite.

"Listen," said Wiggins. "Are you certain sure the ruby's still there? When was the last time you seen it?"

"There's a point," the captain said. "If this professor of crime is so dashed clever, who's to say he hasn't already nipped in here and taken it?"

"Exac'ly," said Wiggins.

The dewan reluctantly agreed to show them the

ruby. He led the way out of the drawing room and down a corridor to a room at the end, which proved to be a study. A leather-topped desk stood in the middle of the room, and the walls were lined with books from floor to ceiling, except for a space in which hung an oil painting of an imposing country mansion. The Boys could see no sign of the ruby anywhere.

To their surprise, the dewan walked over to the picture and swung it away from the wall, to which it was fastened by hinges on one side, like a door. Behind it, set into the wall, was a steel safe. While the others watched, he took the key from round his neck, unlocked the safe and lifted out an ornate golden casket. Carefully, he placed it on the desk and lifted the lid. There was a sigh of relief from everyone. Inside the casket, resting on a bed of dark-blue velvet, was the ruby. It was as big as a small hen's egg, and seemed to glow with a deep red fire. Everyone stared at it in wonder, as though hypnotized.

Uncle Sanjay broke the silence. "There," he said. "The Ranjipur Ruby, all safe and sound."

"At least for now…" said Captain Nicholson.

SIX

"That ruby's the most beautiful thing in the world," Beaver enthused. "You should've seen it."

"Yeah, we should've," Shiner replied peevishly. "We young 'uns always get left out."

"No you don't," Queenie said. "Only when we can't all go."

"Shiner's right," said Gertie. "It ain't fair. You and Wiggins and Beaver get to have all the fun."

"Tell you what," Wiggins said, "why don't we all go to the Bazaar and get Madame Dupont's new leaflets? Then we can hand 'em out together."

"That don't sound like fun to me," Sparrow grumbled. "Sounds more like hard work."

"It is," said Wiggins. "We'll be keeping a lookout for them two Thugs. Only nobody'll know, because they'll think we're just handing out leaflets."

"Good idea," agreed Queenie. "If they're really after Ravi, like as not they'll be hangin' about somewhere, waitin' for a second chance."

"Skulkin'," said Beaver. "That's what they'll be doin'."

"What they got to sulk about?" Shiner asked.

"No, not sulkin' – *skulk*in'," Queenie corrected him. "It's like lurkin', you know. Stayin' out of sight in the shadows."

"Well, whatever they're doing, they'll be keeping their eyes open for Ravi," said Wiggins. "Waiting to do him in."

"We can't have that," cried Gertie. "Come on. Let's get goin'."

There was no sign of Sarge as the Boys trooped past his lodge. He was busy inside and didn't notice them.

"There you are," Wiggins told the others. "He don't see everything, not if he's got something else to do."

"So Moriarty could have slipped in and out without him knowing," said Beaver.

"Exac'ly."

They collected the bag of new leaflets from Madame Dupont, who was still so pleased at the publicity she would get from news of the curse that she agreed to pay them an extra half-crown. Then they headed back to the street. This time Sarge was leaning out over the half-door, putting a match to the black tobacco in his stubby clay pipe.

"Hey, where've you lot been?" he called. "I never seen you come in."

"We've been to see Madame Dupont," Wiggins told him. "You was inside when we passed."

"Ah, right," Sarge replied. "I was busy checking the keys. Just one of me many important duties."

He took half a step back so that they could see a row of keys hanging on hooks inside his door. Each one was neatly labelled, to make sure they did not get mixed up.

"One for every shop and store in the Bazaar," he said proudly. "In case of fire or burglary. I'm responsible for guarding everything when they're closed at night."

He puffed hard at his pipe and almost disappeared behind a cloud of smoke that made the Boys cough and rub their smarting eyes as it reached them.

"You seen any sign of that carriage we was talking about?" Wiggins asked, peering through the smoke and fanning his hand across his face to clear it.

The old soldier shook his head. "Not a whisper," he said. "But I'll keep watching and if it shows up again I'll let you know."

Wiggins thanked him, and the Boys moved off down the street. When they reached the corner, Wiggins handed out bundles of leaflets to each of them and told them where to go. If they spotted anyone or anything suspicious, he said, they were to come and tell him.

It was a gloomy day with a hint of fog in the air. The sooty smell of coal smoke mingled with the stench of manure from the thousands of horses pulling the carts and carriages that packed the main streets. The music from a hurdy-gurdy on a nearby corner was almost drowned out by the noise of wheels and iron-shod hooves on the cobbles. To Wiggins, its tinny melody sounded sad and almost tearful. He hoped this was not a bad omen for the Boys' quest.

When he reached the corner, he saw the organ-grinder turning the hurdy-gurdy's handle, an Italian man in a red velvet jacket and baggy pants. He looked as though he was missing the warm sun of his homeland. The man had a monkey on a lead, also wearing a little velvet jacket, and a tiny hat held on with elastic. When anyone walked past, the little creature held out a tin cup to them, to collect pennies.

Wiggins thought that both the monkey and its owner looked hungry. Knowing that he and the other Boys would eat well that night, he dropped a penny into the cup. He was rewarded with a flashing smile from the Italian and a chatter of teeth from the monkey, which made him feel better. As he walked away down the street, he heard the tune change to something more cheerful. His spirits rose, and so did his hopes.

By the time he had handed out all his leaflets, however, Wiggins had still seen no sign of the two would-be assassins. He had criss-crossed the streets, carefully inspecting every nook and cranny, investigating every doorway and alleyway, but had found nothing. And none of the people he spoke to – crossing-sweepers, window cleaners, messenger boys, cockney costermongers with their barrows piled high with fruit – had seen anything of the men either. It was as if they had simply melted into the crowds that packed London's pavements. Even the fact that they were Indians wearing Indian clothes did not help. In this year of Queen Victoria's diamond jubilee, the city was filled with people from every part of her vast empire, many of them dressed in their national costumes. So there was nothing unusual about two Indians, nothing to make people notice and remember them.

Wearily, Wiggins trudged back to HQ. On the way he met Queenie and Rosie, also heading home. They had seen nothing either. Nor had Beaver and Sparrow, who were already back at HQ. Sparrow said he had spotted an Indian man and had followed him because he looked suspicious.

"How suspicious?" Wiggins wanted to know.

"He kept lookin' round, like he was scared there was somebody followin' him."

"And was there?"

"Only me, far as I could see."

"What was he like?" Wiggins asked.

"Posh," Sparrow answered. "He wasn't dressed

like an Indian. He was wearin' a posh suit and hat, and he had a black cane with a shiny silver knob on top."

"Don't sound much like a Thug to me," said Beaver.

"No," agreed Wiggins. "Anything else special 'bout him?"

"He had a big black moustache. Stuck out either side of his face. Wobbled when he walked."

"Uncle Sanjay!" Wiggins and Beaver exclaimed.

"Who?" asked Sparrow.

"Ravi's uncle," Queenie told him. "No need to worry 'bout him."

"I dare say he was looking round to make sure the Thugs weren't after him," said Wiggins. "Where'd he go?"

"Into a tobacconist's shop," Sparrow said. "I looked in through the window, but he was only buyin' cigars and stuff."

"Well, there you are then. Let's have something to eat, eh?"

It had been a long day, and the Boys were all tired and hungry. Queenie had used Madame Dupont's money to buy the ingredients for one of her special stews — scrag-end of mutton with potatoes and turnips and the like. She set to work preparing it, while Wiggins stoked the fire in the old stove. Beaver took a big enamel jug to the pump in the yard, to fetch water to top up the big stone jar by the stove. He worked the big iron handle up and down until cool water gushed out. It looked so good, he stuck his head under the pump's spout and let it splash over his face, opening his mouth and taking big gulps to quench his thirst.

He had just straightened up and started to fill the jug with water when he heard the sound of running footsteps. A moment later, Shiner appeared, excited and out of breath.

"I seen 'im!" he gasped. "I seen 'im!"

"Who?" asked Beaver. "Who'd you see?"

"Moriarty!"

The Boys gathered round Shiner in great excitement as he began to tell them what he had seen.

"I was walkin' down the street just behind Baker Street station, handin' out leaflets and keepin' my eyes open, like you said. I just give one to this bloke, what was standin' there like he was waitin' for somebody, when this carriage stops right there. And this bloke steps past me and climbs in. I didn't take much notice at first, then all of a sudden I see the sign on the door," he said.

"M!" said Rosie. "M for Moriarty!"

"Who's tellin' this?" Shiner snapped.

"You are," said Queenie. "So just get on with it."

"Could you see who was in the carriage?" Wiggins asked.

"Sort of. He was sat right back in the corner. But it was him right enough. The perfessor."

"How d'you know?" asked Gertie.

"I could see his bald head. Like a big boiled egg it was."

"That's him, all right," Beaver said. "Professor Moriarty his self."

"Well done, Shiner," Wiggins congratulated him. "That proves he really is about."

"Yeah, but we still don't know what he's up to, do we?" Queenie asked.

"Quite right," admitted Wiggins. "We *think* he's after the ruby, but we can't know for sure. Not yet, anyway."

He thought for a moment, then turned back to Shiner.

"Tell me about the other bloke, the one what got into the carriage with him. He wasn't Indian, was he?"

Shiner shook his head. "No," he said. "He was English. A proper toff. But I reckon he was 'ard up."

"How d'you know?"

"His boots. Been mended a few times. Very posh, they was, though – hand made."

"How d'you know that?" Gertie demanded scornfully.

"I know all about boots," said Shiner. "I clean enough of 'em every day. These was good 'uns – but they was very old and worn."

"Like he couldn't afford to buy new ones, you mean?" Wiggins asked.

"Exac'ly." Shiner grinned as he used Wiggins's favourite saying. Wiggins nodded and smiled.

"Well spotted, Shiner," he acknowledged. "We'll make a detective of you yet."

"But we still don't know who he is, do we?" Sparrow insisted. "What good's knowin' he needs new boots if we don't know who he is?"

"But if we did know who he is," Beaver said, "then we'd know he needed new boots and then we'd know he might be a bit hard up, and then we'd know somethin' about him, and then we'd know—"

"Beaver!" Wiggins stopped him before he got completely carried away.

"Oh. Right. Sorry," Beaver apologized.

"S'all right, Beav," Wiggins said. "It could be useful. You never know. Mr Holmes says knowledge is never wasted."

"D'you think we should tell somebody?" Queenie asked.

"No use telling Inspector Lestrade," Wiggins answered. "He'd just say there's nothing illegal in a bloke giving another bloke a ride in his carriage."

"Doctor Watson, then?"

"I dunno. He was a bit put out when the carriage wasn't in the Bazaar. Seems to me the only person worth telling is Mr Holmes – and he's not here to tell."

"Well, let's have some supper first. Then we can think what we're gonna do next."

"I know what *I'm* gonna do," said Sparrow. "I gotta get to the theatre."

Wiggins took his battered old watch from his pocket and consulted it.

"Yeah," he said. "You better get a move on or you'll be late for work. Don't want Mr Trump sacking you again, do we?"

Sparrow pulled a face, and looked hungrily at the stew pot on the stove.

"Don't fret. I'll save you some for when you get home," Queenie told him. "Now, off you go!"

When Sparrow got back from the music hall, most of the others were already fast asleep. Only Wiggins and Queenie were still awake. Queenie had waited up for him, to warm up his supper and be sure he got home safely. She always worried about Sparrow coming back so late on his own, but tonight she was especially worried, knowing that the Thugs were out there somewhere. To be honest, Sparrow had been a bit nervous himself. He did his best not to show it, but he had run most of the way home, avoiding dark doorways and alleyways and hurrying between the pools of light cast by the street lamps.

Wiggins was sitting in his special chair, thinking hard and trying to work out what Moriarty might be planning. He leapt up in alarm as Sparrow came in, puffing and out of breath.

"What's up?" he asked. "Somebody after you?"

"No," Sparrow panted. "I just … wanted to get home. For my supper."

"Oh, right," said Wiggins, knowing that Sparrow wouldn't admit to being scared. He winked at Queenie, who nodded and smiled.

"Here you are then," she said. "I saved it for you, like I promised."

She plonked the plate on the table and gave Sparrow a spoon to eat with.

"Ta. I been waitin' for this all night," he said, tucking in. Running all the way home had given him extra appetite, and he emptied the plate in no time at all. And in no time at all after that, he was snuggled up in bed, fast asleep and dreaming of treasure chests full of fabulous jewels, and banquets of steaming sausages and chops and sticky sweet puddings and ice cream.

Queenie went to her bed as soon as Sparrow was settled, but Wiggins stayed up to think. Eventually he fell asleep in his chair, but he was woken in the middle of the night by the sound of someone entering HQ. Although Wiggins was wide awake in an instant, he could see nothing: the candle by his chair had burnt out, and it was very dark. The intruder seemed to be blundering about, bumping into things. There was a loud clang as Sparrow's empty tin plate was knocked off the table.

"Who's there?" Wiggins asked. "What d'you want?"

"Wiggins?" an urgent voice called. "Is that you? Where are you?"

"Over here. Stand still!"

He found a box of matches, struck one and held it up. By its light he could see someone standing in the middle of the room. It was Ravi.

"Hang on," Wiggins told him. There was a candle on the table, stuck in the neck of a bottle. Wiggins lit it. By the light of its pale flame, he stared at Ravi. The Indian boy looked frightened. His hair was wild and his clothes were untidy and only half fastened.

"Ravi?" Wiggins said. "What is it? What's happened?"

"It's Ram Das," Ravi replied, in a trembling voice. "The dewan. They've murdered him!"

SEVEN

Ravi was still shaking from shock as the rest of the Boys climbed out of their beds and gathered round him. Queenie wrapped him in a blanket and sat him in Wiggins's chair.

"I'll make you some cocoa," she said. "You'll feel better with a nice cup of hot cocoa inside you."

She bustled over to the old black kettle, which was sitting on the stove as usual, singing quietly, and reached for a mug to make a drink for Ravi.

Wiggins crouched down beside the chair and spoke quietly to the young Raja.

"What happened?" he asked.

"I was asleep in my room as usual," Ravi said, "when I was woken by loud noises. It sounded as if things were being knocked over. They came from the dewan's room, which is next to mine. Then there was a scream. A truly terrible scream. It ended suddenly, as though someone was being choked."

He stopped and put his hands over his face, trying to shut out what he had heard and seen. The Boys' faces, pale in the flickering candlelight, reflected the horror of what they were hearing. They were all silent apart from Rosie, who only just managed to stifle a sob.

"So what did you do?" Wiggins asked. "Dive under the bedclothes?"

"No. I heard other people come running, so I went to see for myself. The dewan's door was open. He was lying on the floor. Captain Nicholson was already there, bending over him. One of the maids, Annie, came running along the landing, and William, the footman. But they were all too late."

"The dewan was dead?"

"I'm afraid he … yes, he was."

"How? Could you tell?"

"Captain Nicholson told me. He said he'd been strangled."

The Boys all gasped.

"The Thugs!" said Beaver. "Did they take the key to the safe?"

Ravi shook his head. "No," he said. "It was still round his neck. Captain Nicholson was checking it when Annie and I got there."

"The captain must have scared 'em off," said Queenie. "Before they had time to get the key from him."

"So they had to run for it," said Beaver.

"Empty-handed," said Sparrow.

"That's what Captain Nicholson said. He said there were two of them, but they pushed past him and ran off into the house somewhere. It's a big house."

"And he didn't chase after 'em?" Wiggins asked.

"No. He said he stayed to look after the dewan. But when he saw that he was dead and we were there, he set off to search the house, with William and Mr Hobson."

"Did they find anything?"

"I don't know. I didn't stay to find out."

"You legged it, eh?"

"What?"

"Legged it. You know – scarpered. Vamoosed. Ran for it."

Ravi grinned. Wiggins was pleased to see that he

was recovering from the shock. He was clearly feeling better now that he had his friends around him, and Queenie's cocoa helped too.

"I didn't want to stay in that house with two murderers on the loose," Ravi said. "So I legged it through the kitchen door."

"Don't blame you, mate," said Shiner. "I'd've been outta there quick as a flash."

"Me too," Sparrow agreed.

"Quite so," said Ravi. "Discretion is the better part of valour, as they say!"

"Do they?" asked Rosie, looking puzzled.

"What's that s'posed to mean then?" asked Gertie.

"It means being brave ain't always the best thing to do," Queenie explained.

"Exac'ly," said Ravi, sounding just like Wiggins – who gave him a funny look.

"So you came to us?" Wiggins asked.

"I ran all the way. I feel safe here. You said the Baker Street Boys always look after their friends."

"We do," said Beaver. "You did right, Rav."

"Pity you couldn't have brought the ruby with you," said Wiggins.

"I did the next best thing," said Ravi. He pushed his hand into his pocket and pulled out the key to the safe. "I wasn't going to leave this lying around."

"Where d'you get that?" asked Beaver.

"I took it from the dewan."

"Cor," said Rosie. Like the others, she was deeply impressed that Ravi could have touched a dead body.

"That was brave," said Queenie. "I don't think I could have done that."

"Good lad," said Wiggins. "They can't get at the ruby without that."

"Not unless they got a safe-cracker," said Beaver. "You know – a crook what knows how to open safes. I don't suppose they has safes in India, do they? So they'd have to find a safe-cracker in London, and that'd be hard, 'cos they're strangers here. Course, I dare say Professor Moriarty would know somebody, but then they don't know Professor Moriarty, do they? Mind, we don't know that for sure—"

"Beaver!" cried Wiggins. "Hold it! I'm trying to think."

He began pacing across the floor. He had his thoughtful face on again, and he stroked his chin as he paced. The others watched him, and waited. At last he stopped, and turned to face them, looking serious.

"What if…" he said, "what if it weren't the ruby they was after."

"What d'you mean?" asked Shiner. "It's worth a fortune. You said so."

"Yeah, it is. But Ravi didn't have it with him when they tried to strangle him in Clarke's Court, did he?"

The others stared at Wiggins, trying to fathom out what he meant. But Ravi knew.

"You're absolutely right, old chap," he told him. "They couldn't have been after the ruby that time."

"You said the dewan's room was next to yours," Wiggins went on.

"You think they went into the wrong room in the dark?"

"Could have."

"So they killed Ram Das by mistake?"

"Exac'ly."

"You mean it was me they really wanted to kill."

There was silence for a moment as the rest of the Boys took this in.

"The curse of the Ranjipur Ruby strikes again,"

said Beaver lugubriously. "Or at least it would have, if Ravi had been in the other room, or the dewan had been in his, or if it hadn't been so dark, 'cos now that Ravi's dad's dead—"

"Beaver!" Queenie stopped him.

"Sorry. I didn't mean ... I mean I didn't want to upset Ravi about his dad..."

"It's quite all right," Ravi reassured him. "My father and I were never very close," he explained. "He was always off shooting things, or playing polo or visiting other princes. So I never saw much of him."

"Course, that's only an idea," said Wiggins. "They *could* have been after the ruby. We know how much they want it. They could have killed the dewan to get the key." He paused as another thought entered his mind, then went on: "But how'd they know he'd got it?"

"P'raps Moriarty told 'em," said Beaver. "He knows *everythin'*."

The others nodded gloomily. It did seem as though their arch-enemy was always ahead of them, and always shrouded in mystery.

"Yeah, but who told Moriarty?" Wiggins asked.

"If we could find that out, we'd find the murderer."

"How we gonna do that?" asked Queenie.

Wiggins shook his head. "Dunno," he replied. "Not yet, anyway."

"Well, what *are* we gonna do?"

"I know what I'd like to do," said Ravi. "I'd like to stay here with you. May I?"

The Boys looked at each in surprise. Ravi was rich and could live anywhere in comfort. Why would he want to join them in a draughty old cellar where they never had enough to eat? Besides which, what could he do to earn his keep? He wouldn't be much good at foraging for food or doing odd jobs – no one could imagine him sweeping crossings or holding horses' heads. On the other hand, Shiner thought, the Boys' first rule was that they shared everything; if Ravi were to share his money with them, none of them would ever have to do any of those jobs again.

Wiggins, however, had other thoughts. "You'd be very welcome, Ravi old son," he said. "But I don't think it'd be a good idea. When they realize you're missing, your uncle and Captain Nicholson and everybody'll start looking for you. And it won't take long afore they twig where you are. They know we're your friends. You ain't got no other friends in London, have you?"

Ravi shook his head glumly. Wiggins went on.

"Like as not they'll get the coppers in on the hunt. And even old Lestrade might be able to put two and two together and reckon as you're with us."

"But this place, HQ, it's secret."

"And we'd like to keep it that way."

"Wiggins is right," Queenie said. "It's only secret because the coppers have never had to look for it."

"If they did," Beaver joined in, "it wouldn't take 'em long. They know we live round 'ere somewhere."

"You see," said Wiggins, "they wouldn't bother with most folks, but seeing as how you're a prince, they won't stop till they find you."

Breakfast was barely on the table at Number 221b Baker Street next morning when Wiggins rang the doorbell. He and the other Boys had spent most of the night wondering what they should do. If Mr Holmes had not been away, they would have hurried round to ask his advice: he would certainly have known what to do. Finally, they had decided that in his absence they would have to talk to Dr Watson, even though he had doubted them over the business of Professor Moriarty's carriage.

A bleary-eyed Billy opened the door and glared at the three scruffy street urchins standing on the step.

"Not you lot again," he growled. "What do you want, disturbing decent people at this time of day?"

"We wanna see Dr Watson," Wiggins said. "That's if Mr Holmes still ain't back."

"No, he ain't," said Billy. He stared at them, curious that one of them seemed to have a very dark face beneath the tattered cap pulled low over his eyes.

"And who's he?" he demanded, pointing at Ravi.

"That's none of your business," Wiggins replied.

"It is if I'm letting him into this house," Billy shot back. "Mrs Hudson's very particular about who we let in."

Beaver leant towards him confidentially and spoke quietly.

"This is the Raja of Ranjipur," he said.

"Oh, yeah?" Billy shot back, grinning at the ragged figure standing before him. "And I'm the Prince of Wales. Get out of here!"

Ravi stepped forward and gave the pageboy a haughty stare.

"My name is Prince Ravindranatharam and I am the Raja of Ranjipur," he said in a lordly voice. "Now, boy, hurry along and inform Dr Watson that my friends and I wish to speak with him on a matter of great urgency."

Billy's mouth dropped open at the tone of Ravi's command. He stood rooted to the spot until Ravi clapped his hands imperiously and ordered: "At once, miserable boy!" Then he scuttled away as fast as he could, to the delight of Wiggins and Beaver.

Dr Watson was in his dressing gown again when Billy showed in his three visitors.

"I shall have to start getting up earlier if this goes on!" he greeted them. "What is it this time? Have you seen our friend Professor Moriarty again?"

"Yes," said Wiggins. "As a matter of fact we have. But that ain't why we're here."

"We're here because there's been a murder done," Beaver told him.

"Oh, dear," said Dr Watson. "Not your friend Ravi, I hope?"

"No, guv'nor. This is Ravi."

Ravi smiled at him and held out his hand.

"How do you do, Doctor," he said. "I'm glad to meet you."

Dr Watson shook his hand but stared in puzzlement at the Indian boy's ragged clothes and his face carefully smudged with dirt.

"But why…?" he asked. "Why is he dressed like that?"

"We thought it advisable," Ravi said, "with Thugs and murderers on the loose."

"I see," said the doctor, looking as though he didn't see at all.

"So I lent him some clobber," Wiggins said.

"The Boys thought my normal clobber would have drawn attention to me when we were legging it along the street," Ravi explained.

"And we didn't want that," Beaver added. "Not with them two bloodthirsty Thugs on the lookout for him after they killed the dewan by mistake."

"Course, we don't know that for sure," Wiggins said. "They could have been after the ruby."

"Only, the dewan had the key round his neck," said Beaver. "So they couldn't get it 'less they done him in. See, if he hadn't had the key round his neck, and if it hadn't been pitch dark in the house in the middle of the night so they couldn't tell Ravi's room from the dewan's—"

"Stop! Stop!" Dr Watson cried, shaking his head in confusion. "Now you really have lost me. Perhaps you'd better sit down and start at the beginning."

So, with the help of Ravi and the occasional hindrance of Beaver, Wiggins explained all that had happened. Dr Watson listened carefully, looking more and more serious as the tale progressed. When Ravi described seeing the dewan's body lying on the floor, he let out a low whistle.

"My goodness," he said. "That must have been terrible for you. No wonder you took fright and ran away."

"That's right," said Ravi. "I legged it as fast as I could, round to my friends at HQ."

"Hmmm," said Dr Watson. "I'm not sure that was the wisest thing to do, but never mind, you came to no harm and here you are."

"The thing is, guv'nor," Wiggins said, "what do we do with Ravi now?"

"Oh, there can be no question about that," the

doctor told him. "He must go home."

"Back to that house?"

"It will be quite safe. It's daylight now, and the police will be there. I've no doubt they'll have searched the house from top to bottom."

"Do I have to?" Ravi pleaded.

"Your uncle and your tutor will have been worried sick about you. They're not to know you haven't been abducted, or worse. You must go back at once, and face the music."

EIGHT

There was a large, comforting London bobby standing guard outside Lord Holdhurst's house when the
Boys and Ravi arrived. At first he did not want to
let them go up to the front door, but fortunately Dr
Watson had come with them, and he was soon able
to convince the policeman that Ravi really was a
prince, in spite of his scruffy appearance, and that
he lived there. But when Annie, the maid, opened
the door and saw him, she found it hard not to
laugh.

"Ooh, Prince Ravi!" she exclaimed. "I wouldn't
have recognized you in them togs."

"That's good," Wiggins said. "If *you* didn't know
him, then maybe the Thugs wouldn't neither."

"Where have you been?" Annie asked Ravi.
"Everybody's been going frantic trying to find you."

"Never mind that," said Ravi. "Did they find the murderers?"

"No, sir. There wasn't any sign of them in the house. They got clean away."

"How did they escape? Does anybody know?"

"Captain Nicholson found a window open upstairs. He says they must have got out that way and jumped down to the street. But how they got in is a mystery. Mr Hobson says all the doors were locked tight."

"I see. Where is the captain now?"

"In the drawing room, sir, with your uncle. They've got a policeman with them."

"Excellent. Come on, chaps. We'll go right up." And he raced up the stairs, calling back over his shoulder, "Oh, this is Dr Watson, by the way. He's our friend."

Dr Watson smiled at Annie, handed her his top hat and cane and followed the three boys up the stairs rather more slowly. Annie watched them go, shaking her head in disbelief.

Inside the drawing room, Captain Nicholson and Uncle Sanjay gasped in surprise as Ravi burst through the door and rushed in.

"What the Dickens…?" the captain exclaimed.

"What is the meaning of this intrusion?" Uncle Sanjay asked indignantly. "Who is this ruffian?"

"It's me!" Ravi shouted. "Ravi!"

"It is I," Captain Nicholson corrected him automatically. "Good heavens! Where on earth have you been?"

"And what are you doing in those disgusting clothes?" Uncle Sanjay asked, wrinkling his nose as though he detected a bad smell.

"Do I take it that this is the missing prince?" There was a third man in the room, standing with his back to the fireplace. Inspector Lestrade. He stared in amazement at Ravi, then groaned when Wiggins and Beaver followed him into the room.

"Oh, no," he sighed. "I might have known you lot would have a hand in all this."

"Morning, Inspector," said Wiggins cheerfully. "Glad to see you're on the case."

"I am," said the inspector. "And don't you forget it. Oh, I see Dr Watson's with you! Good morning, Doctor. What brings you here?"

"I'm making sure Prince Ravi is safe."

"No Mr Holmes?"

"No. He is away, on a case."

The doctor introduced himself to Captain Nicholson and Uncle Sanjay. He explained how he came to be involved, and how he had accompanied Ravi and the Boys to make sure they got him home safely.

"I thank you, Doctor," said Uncle Sanjay. "You acted wisely."

"Which is more than can be said of our young prince," said Captain Nicholson sternly. "What on earth were you thinking of, Ravi, disappearing like that?"

"I was scared," said Ravi. "Those geezers had already tried to do me in once."

"That's right," said Wiggins, giving Inspector Lestrade a hard look. "If it hadn't been for us..."

The inspector gave a loud cough.

"Yes, yes," he said testily. "We are now investigating a real murder. Not some fabrication about a phantom professor."

"It weren't a fabri-whatsit," said Beaver. "Our friend Shiner seen him again yesterday."

"Who?" asked Captain Nicholson.

"The professor. Moriarty. And he ain't no ghost."

"I can vouch for that, Inspector," said Dr Watson. "And so can Mr Holmes. Professor Moriarty may be the Devil incarnate, but I assure you he's as real as you or I."

"And what exactly did your young friend see?" the inspector asked sarcastically. "Another empty carriage?"

"No. This time he seen the professor his self, sittin' in it. And he stopped to pick up somebody else."

"Did he get a good look at the other man?" Captain Nicholson asked.

"Yeah. But he didn't know who he was, 'ceptin' he was a toff."

"But would he recognize him if he saw him again?"

"Course he would. He's bright as a button is our Shiner. Don't miss a thing."

The captain nodded thoughtfully.

"What has this Moriarty person to do with the murder of Mr Ram Das?" asked Uncle Sanjay. "Are you suggesting that he killed him?"

"Oh, no," Wiggins replied. "The professor's the

brains. He gets other people to do the dirty work while he lurks in the shadows, pulling the strings. Ain't that right, Doctor?"

"That is how it appears to be," Dr Watson agreed.

"Skulkin'," said Beaver dramatically.

Lestrade cleared his throat again. "That's all very fanciful," he said. "Like something from the pages of a penny dreadful. But we are dealing with reality here, not make-believe."

"Quite right, Inspector," said the captain. "I think we've heard enough of this nonsense."

"It's not nonsense," Ravi cried. "You must listen to them!"

"What we have here," the inspector said impatiently, "is a failed robbery. A jewel robbery that went wrong, with tragic results. Nothing more."

"Which reminds me," the captain said to Ravi. "The key. I presume you took it from poor Ram Das's body?"

"Yes, I did."

"Why?"

"To keep it safe."

"While you ran around the streets of London in

the middle of the night? Really, Ravi, that was not very clever of you."

"I thought the murderers might still be in the house. I ran to the Baker Street Boys' hide-out. The Thugs would never find me there."

"Well, you are not to go there again. Ever. Do you hear me?"

Ravi glowered at his tutor but said nothing. The captain went on.

"These boys are not suitable companions for you. You are not to see them again."

"They are my friends. I'll see them if I want to!"

"That's enough! You are not to set foot outside this house without your uncle or me. And your so-called friends are not to come here again. Now go to your room and get changed out of those revolting rags. I'll tell Annie to run you a bath – no doubt you need one. But first, hand over the key. I'll take care of it now."

He held out his hand. But Ravi did not move. Instead, he stood up very straight and looked the captain in the eye.

"Captain Nicholson," he said coldly, "you are forgetting who I am. Now that my father is dead, I am the Raja of Ranjipur – and, until I present it to Her Majesty Queen Victoria, the ruby belongs to me. So I will keep the key."

The captain glared at Ravi as though he would like to box his ears. But with both Inspector Lestrade and Dr Watson watching, there was nothing he could do except back down. He lowered his head slightly in a curt little bow. Uncle Sanjay nodded and gave Ravi a rather oily smile.

"His Highness is totally correct," he said. "He most certainly is the Raja."

"As you say," the captain agreed through gritted teeth.

"I do say," said Uncle Sanjay. "Now, Ravi my boy, why don't you run along and have your bath, and then you can put on some more suitable attire?"

When Dr Watson left them and headed back towards Number 221b, Wiggins and Beaver stood on the pavement outside the house and looked back up at the windows. They seemed very high, and Wiggins wondered how anyone could have jumped down into the street without breaking a leg or at least an ankle. And in any case, they would have had to jump outwards as well as down: on either side of the steps to the front door was the basement kitchen area, fenced off from the pavement by black-painted iron railings topped with fierce spikes, like spears.

"I wouldn't like to take my chances of missing them spikes," Wiggins told Beaver.

"They could have been acrobats, like in the circus," Beaver said. "If they was used to the flying trapeze…" He tailed off as Wiggins gave him a withering glance.

The policeman on duty outside the house plodded towards them.

"Now then, lads," he said. "You can't hang about here. Clear off."

Wiggins was about to tell him that he was not hanging about but investigating a murder. But he thought better of it, and pulled Beaver away round the corner. The house had no basement here and no dangerous railings, but the only windows were very high up and he doubted if even an acrobat would have dared to leap from them.

He thought about the problem all the way home, hardly speaking a word to Beaver. He was so engrossed in his thoughts that he did not notice the

Italian organ-grinder's monkey rattling his tin cup at him in the hope of another penny. And he did not hear the cheery greetings of their friends in the street. But by the time they got back to HQ, Wiggins had the beginnings of a plan.

"There's something very peculiar about this murder," Wiggins told the other Boys. "Nobody knows how the killers got into the house. And I don't see how they could have got out of it, neither."

He held the lapels of his coat and looked hard at his audience, waiting for someone to say something.

"P'raps they didn't," suggested Queenie.

"P'raps somebody helped them," said Rosie.

"Exac'ly!" Wiggins replied. "Either way, it could have been what they calls an inside job."

"Inside what?" asked Shiner.

"Inside the house of course, stupid," said Sparrow.

"Sure and don't we all know that?" said Gertie, sounding particularly Irish. "Wasn't he in his bedroom when he was murdered, poor fella?"

"Who you callin' stupid?" Shiner squared up to Sparrow, giving him a shove in the chest.

"Hold it! Hold it, both of you," said Wiggins. "It don't mean that at all. What it means is, the crime was done by somebody who was in the house, somebody who has what they calls 'inside knowledge'."

There was silence as the other Boys took this in.

"Unless there was somebody in the house what let 'em in," Beaver suggested.

"And locked up again after they done it," said Sparrow.

"What, with everybody rushin' about all over the place?" asked Queenie.

"Exac'ly!" said Wiggins.

"So who done it?" asked Beaver. "You think p'raps it was that butler? He didn't like the look of us, did he?"

"I didn't like the look of *him*," Wiggins grinned. "Snooty old so-and-so. But that don't make him a murderer."

"Well, who is, then?"

"I dunno. All we know for sure is that somebody in that house is either the murderer or in league with the murderers. If I could question everybody, I reckon I'd soon find out who. But we ain't allowed back in there, so I can't."

"What we gonna do, then?" Queenie asked.

"We're gonna keep an eye on 'em from outside. Watch to see who goes in and who comes out, and where they go."

"But won't they spot us?"

"They'd spot you and me and Beaver, 'cos they know us. But they ain't seen Sparrow, nor Shiner, nor Rosie, nor Gertie. So they don't know them. Now, Shiner, I want you to take your box with your brushes and polish, and set yourself up opposite the front door. And Rosie, you take your tray of flowers and work the other side of the street."

"What about Gertie and me?" asked Sparrow. "What'll *we* do?"

"We got a few of Madame Dupont's leaflets left. You can be handing those out. I'll go see if she's got any more."

"Right!"

"If you see anything interesting, come and report to me. But make sure there's always at least one of you on sentry duty."

Fired with fresh enthusiasm now they had something useful to do, the younger Boys collected their things and hurried off to their posts.

Madame Dupont was happy to give Wiggins more leaflets, especially when he said the Boys would not want to be paid for distributing them.

"I'm a bit busy just now, dearie," she told him brightly, "but you remember where they are, don't you? Help yourselves – there's plenty there."

Wiggins and Beaver walked through the exhibition to the far corner of the gallery and found the hidden door. It opened quite easily. Just inside the dark storeroom was a pile of neatly wrapped parcels containing the new leaflets. Behind them in the gloom they could just make out a clutter of odds and ends and the dim shapes of old waxwork figures loosely covered with dust sheets. There was something spooky about these human shapes standing so still and silent, and the two Boys were glad to take a parcel of leaflets each and leave.

Walking back through the streets to his watchers, Wiggins was happy to be investigating again. He found a penny for the organ-grinder's monkey, and stopped a little further on to pat two great shire horses standing patiently at the kerbside, attached to a heavy coal cart. The coalman, wearing a leather helmet with a long flap that stretched down behind him to his waist, was lifting the heavy sacks down from the cart onto his back, then bending forward to empty them through a circular hole in the pavement into the house cellar below.

As he swept the spilled coal dust into the hole before replacing the ornate cast-iron cover, the coalman gave Wiggins a friendly greeting. The Boys knew him well – he sometimes managed to "accidentally" spill a few lumps of coal into the gutter, which they could salvage and carry back to HQ. Today, however, Wiggins was too busy to bother with collecting fuel. He had more important things to do, and he went on his way with a quick wave.

At first, the four Boys watching the outside of Lord Holdhurst's house found their task quite exciting. But as the hours passed and nothing unusual happened, time began to drag. A posh grocer's van, drawn by a high-stepping black horse with a glossy coat, brought baskets of food, which were carried down the steps to the kitchen door in the basement by a delivery man with a long white apron over his green uniform. The postman called twice, to push letters through the front door. And once, a telegraph boy pedalled up the street on his red bicycle, rang the doorbell and handed over a telegram in a buff envelope. But the Boys had no way of knowing if the message he brought was urgent or if it had anything to do with Ravi or the murder.

"I'm bored," Shiner grumbled to Rosie as she walked past him with her little tray of posies. "I ain't had a single customer all the time I've been 'ere."

"No," Rosie agreed. "I ain't done much better."

"If I'd been in the station, I'd have done half a dozen shines," he went on. "*And* got paid for 'em."

"Yeah, but that ain't why we're here, is it?"

"Waste of time, if you ask me. Ain't nothin' gonna happen."

Rosie was inclined to agree with Shiner but said nothing. It was getting dark, and her empty stomach was starting to rumble. Shortly afterwards, however, the front door opened and the portly figure of Uncle Sanjay appeared. He trotted down the steps and set off along the street. Sparrow and Gertie signalled to each other and set off after him, keeping a little way behind but making sure they did not lose sight of him. He turned off the main street and entered a shop.

"Same as last time," Sparrow told Gertie. "He'll only be buyin' his cigars again."

"Better keep an eye on him all the same," said Gertie.

They waited outside the shop until Uncle Sanjay came out, carrying a small paper bag. To their surprise, he did not head back towards the house but hurried off in the opposite direction. They followed, cautiously, and saw him turn into a back street, where he stopped at one of the mean little houses, knocked at the door and went in.

"Now what would a bloke like him want in a house like that?" Gertie asked.

"Search me," said Sparrow. "Let's go and take a look."

They strolled nonchalantly over to the house and then, glancing around to make sure nobody was watching them, crept up to the window and peeped inside. The gaslight had been lit in the room. Through the grimy glass and a tattered lace curtain, they could see Uncle Sanjay speaking to someone out of their sight. They saw him take a large packet of cigarettes from the paper bag and place it on the table in the middle of the room. Then he put his hand in his pocket, pulled out a purse, and counted out a small pile of coins. As the Boys watched, two men stepped forward into view, to pick up the money.

"It's them!" Sparrow gasped. "It's the Thugs!"

NINE

"What was they like, these two geezers?" Wiggins asked. "Was they English?"

"No," said Sparrow. "Not 'less they been out in the sun."

"Indians, I'd say," said Gertie.

"They was wearin' long shirts."

"Outside their pants."

"Baggy pants," said Sparrow.

"Cotton. Grey cotton," Gertie added. "And bits of cloth wrapped round their heads."

"Turbans," said Beaver.

"Sounds like our blokes," said Queenie.

Wiggins nodded. Sparrow and Gertie had hurried back to HQ to report, after following Uncle Sanjay back to Lord Holdhurst's house, where Shiner and Rosie were still on guard. They were buzzing with excitement at what they had discovered.

"Anything else about 'em?" Wiggins asked.

"Well," said Sparrow, "one of 'em had a dirty great scar on his face."

"All the way from his eyebrow to his chin," added Gertie.

"That settles it," said Wiggins. "They're the Thugs what tried to do Ravi in."

"But what's his Uncle Sanjay doin', givin' them money?" asked Queenie.

The Boys stared at each other, aghast, as they realized the awful truth. There could be only one explanation.

"He was paying their wages," said Wiggins. "They're working for him!"

"You mean he paid 'em to murder Ravi?" asked Beaver. "Why'd he do that? I mean, he's his uncle."

Wiggins took a deep breath and shook his head in exasperation. How could the others not see something that seemed so obvious to him? On the other hand, he thought more kindly, how had he himself not seen it before?

"It's like this," he explained. "Ravi's the Raja, right? And Sanjay's his uncle. So, if anything should happen to Ravi, who gets to be the next Raja?"

"Uncle Sanjay!" the others shouted in unison, amazed once again at their leader's brilliance. Only Beaver still looked puzzled.

"Hang on," he said. "When they tried to kill Ravi the first time, he wasn't the Raja yet. His dad was."

"No, Ravi was," Wiggins replied. "His dad was already dead – only nobody knew it."

"Uncle Sanjay did," said Queenie. "He was in Scotland with him."

There was another silence as they all considered this and thought about what it might mean. At last, Wiggins spoke again.

"Oh, my oath!" he said. "He must have killed Ravi's dad – or had him killed by them two thugs. Then sent 'em back here to do Ravi in."

"But I thought the Thugs was s'posed to kill people for their goddess, Kali," said Gertie. "Like a sacrifice."

"Or in revenge for stealin' the ruby," Sparrow added.

"Yeah," said Wiggins. "That's what we're s'posed to think. That way, nobody'd suspect Uncle Sanjay, would they?"

"Oh, that is diabolical," said Queenie.

"I bet they ain't even real Thugs," said Beaver. "I bet they're only pretending to be. I bet that's what that sugar was for – to make people think they was real Thugs."

"Course they ain't real Thugs," Wiggins interrupted him. "Like everybody says, the real Thugs was stamped out fifty years ago. This lot are just killers working for Uncle Sanjay."

"We gotta warn Ravi," said Queenie. "They've had two goes at him already. We stopped 'em first time. The second time it was Captain Nicholson. If they try again, it might be third time lucky."

"How we gonna stop 'em?" asked Sparrow.

"The captain. We gotta tell him. Now."

Wiggins headed for the door, but before he got there Shiner came through it, out of breath and wild-eyed.

"Shiner?" Queenie said. "What is it? What's up?"

"It's him!" Shiner gasped. "The bloke what was with Moriarty. The bloke with the boots. I seen him comin' out of the house. He lives there!"

"Who is he? What's he look like?" Wiggins asked.

"Tall, near enough six foot. Light hair, fair moustache…"

Wiggins, Beaver and Queenie stared at each other in horror. There was only one person in the house who fitted that description.

"Captain Nicholson!" said Wiggins. "Oh, my word … he's in on it. Now what do we do?"

"We can't leave Ravi in that house with the captain and Uncle Sanjay," said Queenie. "We gotta get him out."

"Yeah, right," said Beaver. "But how?"

They all turned to Wiggins for an answer.

"I'll have to think," he said.

"Well don't take too long," said Queenie. "We gotta get to him afore the stranglers do."

Wiggins paced the floor. He put on his old deer-stalker hat, and even sucked on his curly pipe. He sat in his special chair and thought hard. But still he couldn't see how they could get into Lord Hold-hurst's house to rescue Ravi.

As Sparrow left for his job at the theatre, Rosie came in, cold and hungry. Shiner said he felt like he had a big hole where his stomach ought to be, and could he have something to eat. Queenie told him to bring in a fresh lump of coal from their little pile in the yard outside, to stoke up the stove so that she could start cooking.

As Shiner dropped the coal into the stove, Wiggins suddenly sat up. Seeing it reminded him of the coalman, emptying his bags into the hole in the pavement. And the hole in the pavement made him think of cellars, and cellars made him think of underground passages. What was it that Sarge had said about Lord Holdhurst's father, who built the Bazaar? That he used to pop up from nowhere, inside the Bazaar, so he could keep an eye on things. And nobody knew how he got there, but there was talk about underground tunnels. He must have had a tunnel from his house, which was right behind the gallery that now housed Madame Dupont's waxworks.

"That's it!" he cried, leaping to his feet. "I know how they got in."

"How?" everybody wanted to know.

"There's a secret passage. From Madame Dupont's waxworks."

"How d'you know that?" Beaver asked.

"Tell you later. We ain't got time now."

"But if it's secret, how come the thugs knowed about it?"

"Moriarty," said Wiggins. "He'd know about it."

"Moriarty knows everythin'," said Shiner gloomily.

"But does he know we're on his trail?" asked Gertie.

"He does now," said Wiggins. "We told the captain – and the captain's in league with him."

"Oh, lawks," said Queenie. "What we gonna do?"

"We got no time to lose," Wiggins said. "You go and see Dr Watson. Take Shiner with you, and Gertie. They can tell him what they seen the captain and Uncle Sanjay doing. And tell him Beaver and me and Rosie are going into the house through the secret tunnel in the Bazaar."

He hurried over to the shelf in the corner and lifted down his bull's-eye lantern.

"We're gonna need this," he said. "It'll be dark in there."

"But where exac'ly is this tunnel?" asked Beaver.

"I dunno yet. But if it's there, we'll find it. Queenie, tell Dr Watson to send for Inspector Lestrade, quick as he can. Right, everybody – let's go!"

It was dark and the evening fog was swirling through the streets as the Boys left HQ on their missions to save Ravi. Queenie, Shiner and Gertie ran up Baker Street to 221b, but when they finally managed to persuade Billy to open the door, he told them the doctor was out and he didn't know when he would be back. This left them with a quandary. They could make their way to Scotland Yard on their own, but without Dr Watson they knew that Inspector Lestrade probably wouldn't listen to them. They decided that all they could do was wait on the doorstep.

Wiggins, Beaver and Rosie, meanwhile, hurried to the Bazaar. But when they arrived they found that Madame Dupont's waxworks were locked up for the night. And there was no sign of Sarge in his lodge.

"Where could he be?" Rosie asked.

"He's probably took his jug down the pub to get some beer," said Wiggins. "He does like a quiet pint of an evening."

"Yeah, but we need him here," said Beaver. "How else are we gonna get into Madame Dupont's?"

"Easy," said Wiggins. "Look." He pushed open the door of the lodge and shone the beam of his lantern on the rows of keys hanging on the wall. Each key was neatly labelled, and it didn't take him long to find the one they needed. They ran past the shops and the parked carriages, the sound of their footsteps on the cobbles echoing through the empty Bazaar, and in no time Wiggins was unlocking the doors of the gallery.

"Quiet, now," he told the others. "You never know who might be around."

Inside, the Red Indian brave looked more menacing than ever in the dark hallway, and, as the Boys tiptoed through the gallery, the glassy eyes of all the wax models seemed to watch every step they took. Most of the gaslights were turned off, but two or three were still burning, very low, leaving big patches of deep shadow.

"It's scary in here," Rosie whispered, staying close to Beaver.

"What we lookin' for?" Beaver asked. "D'you think it might be a trapdoor or somethin'?"

"Could be. Whatever it is, it's probably hidden."

"That room where Madame Dupont kept the

leaflets was hidden," said Rosie. "You wouldn't have thought there was a door there if you didn't know."

"That's right," said Beaver. "It looked like part of the panellin' till she pushed it."

"Good thinking, Rosie," Wiggins congratulated the little flower girl. "C'mon, let's take a look."

They moved quickly to the hidden door and pushed it open. Behind it, the storeroom looked dark and forbidding. They crept inside nervously and looked around by the light of Wiggins's lantern. The wax figures under their dust sheets looked even more sinister than Wiggins remembered, and Rosie clung to Beaver's sleeve, trying desperately not to scream as she thought she saw one of them move.

"It's all right," Wiggins reassured her. "They can't hurt you. They ain't real people."

"I know that," Rosie squeaked. "But they're still scary."

"Don't you fret. Beaver and me'll look after you."

But a moment later they all jumped as something in the room really *did* move. Wiggins swung the light towards the sound and they all sighed with relief as they saw a little grey mouse skitter across the floor and dive into its hole in the wall.

The mouse hole, though, seemed to be the only opening in the wall. There were no doors or windows. But when Wiggins walked over to the far corner of the room he discovered something else.

"Found it!" he cried triumphantly. "Look, Beav – there it is." And indeed it was. A small iron ring set into the floorboards betrayed the presence of a square trapdoor. Wiggins stared at it for a moment, then took a deep breath, grabbed hold of the ring and pulled. Nothing happened.

"It's a bit stiff," he groaned. "Come on, Beav, give us a hand."

The trapdoor was too heavy for Wiggins to lift on his own, but when Beaver added his strength they were able to pull it up together and lean it against the wall. Beneath it, a flight of stone steps led down into a deep black hole. The Boys looked at each other and gulped. It would take every bit of their nerve to climb down into it. But they knew they had to – Ravi's life was at stake.

Full of apprehension, they set off, Wiggins leading the way with the lantern. At the bottom of the steps, the floor levelled out into a tunnel, stretching before them into a threatening darkness. The air smelt dank and musty. The walls and floor were dripping with moisture. Black beetles scuttled away from the light, and Beaver was sure he heard the high-pitched squeaking of rats ahead of them. Wiggins could not help crying out as cobwebs as thick as knitting wool wrapped themselves round his face. He tried to brush them off, then stopped and turned back to the others.

"These cobwebs ain't been disturbed for years," he said.

"No," Beaver agreed. "They're real thick, ain't they."

"No, what I'm saying is, nobody's been in this tunnel lately."

"But what about the thugs?" Beaver asked. "How did they get into the house, then?"

"I dunno. P'raps they didn't."

"What d'you mean?"

"P'raps it weren't the thugs what murdered the dewan."

"If it weren't the thugs, who was it?"

"The captain," said Wiggins. "Gotta be."

"You mean he was tellin' lies when he said he'd seen the killers?"

"Right. He thought he could do it quiet like, with the handkerchief, and nobody would know till they found the body in the morning. But he wasn't quick enough, and the old bloke got out a scream afore he snuffed it."

"And that woke everybody up."

"Exac'ly. When Annie found him bending over the body, he hadn't just disturbed the killers, like he said. He'd just killed the dewan."

"The villain! We better hurry up and get Ravi out of that house."

"Can we hurry up and get ourselves out of this tunnel?" asked Rosie, who had not said a word since they climbed down through the trapdoor. "I don't like it down here."

"No more do I," said Wiggins. "Come on, then. All stick close together."

He pushed on, through more cobwebs. Beaver followed, with Rosie hanging onto his coat. Soon they reached another flight of steps, going up. At the top was a solid door. Wiggins turned the handle and pushed at the door. It had not been used for a very long time and was as heavy and stiff as the trapdoor at the other end. As it opened, it creaked alarmingly. The noise sounded very loud in the tunnel. The three Boys froze, holding their breath and listening for any sound from the other side. After what seemed an age, Wiggins turned back to the others.

"Can't hear nothing," he whispered. "We'll have to chance it."

He pushed the door again, very carefully, moving it only a little at a time. When the opening was wide enough, he peered through into a darkened room, and when he was sure there was no one there he slipped inside and beckoned the others to follow. They stood huddled together as he swung the beam from the bull's-eye lantern around the room. It looked familiar to Wiggins.

"I know where this is," he whispered. "It's His Lordship's study. But I don't remember this door."

Beaver and Rosie crept through the door after Wiggins and looked around them at the book-lined walls. The door they had just come through was part of the shelves, complete with books. When it was closed it would be invisible, looking no different from the rest of the bookshelves. Only one leather-bound book was not real: now that the door was open, they could see that when it was pulled forward, this book worked the handle. Wiggins fingered it thoughtfully. No wonder no one knew about the tunnel.

"That's clever," he said, and looked around him curiously. With the picture hiding the safe, and now the bookshelves concealing the door to the tunnel, he wondered what other secrets the room held. He would have loved to explore it to find out, but he knew there was no time.

"Where do we go now?" Rosie asked. "How do we find Ravi?"

"We have to look in all the rooms till we find his."

"But what if we open the wrong door and somebody sees us?" asked Beaver.

"And what do we do if we bump into the captain?" Rosie wanted to know.

"We just have to be very, very careful. Come on, now."

Wiggins tiptoed over to the door into the corridor, beckoning the others to follow. But as he stretched out his hand to grasp the doorknob, it turned. The door began to open. They would never get back to the secret tunnel before whoever was on the other side came into the room and caught them. The door swung open. Wiggins tried to hide behind it and pull the others in with him. But there was no room, and no time. They were trapped.

TEN

The person entering the study was carrying an oil lamp and a book. The lamp's gentle glow lit up the small room – and with it the three Boys, who were desperately trying to hide behind the door. It also lit up the face of the person carrying it.

"Annie!" Wiggins blurted out, greatly relieved. The young maid let out a small scream, but stopped as he darted forward and put his hand lightly over her mouth.

"Ssh!" he hushed her. "It's all right. It's us, the Baker Street Boys."

He reached out and closed the door quietly behind her.

"Ooh!" she cried, putting the lamp and the book down on the desk. "You could have frightened me to death. How did you get in? The house is all locked up for the night."

Wiggins pointed to the door in the bookshelves. "Secret passage," he said.

"Gracious me!" Annie exclaimed. "I never knew about that. But why? What are you doing here?"

"We've come to save Ravi," Wiggins told her. "He's in terrible danger."

"You'll be in danger too if Captain Nicholson or Prince Sanjay catch you. They'll 'ave you locked up."

"I dare say they'd do worse than that," said Beaver. "It's them as is plottin' to kill Ravi."

"What on earth are you talking about?"

"It wasn't the thugs what murdered the dewan," said Wiggins. "It was Captain Nicholson. And Prince Sanjay's in it with him."

"How do you know that?"

"I ain't got time to tell you now, but it's true. We gotta get Ravi out the house afore they does him in."

"But ... the *captain*?"

"Listen – when you found him with the body, did you see anybody else?"

"No. Only the captain. He said he'd disturbed the murderers."

"So why wasn't he chasing after 'em?"

"I don't know."

"'Cos they wasn't there, that's why. It was him!"

Annie's mouth dropped open. "But why?" she asked.

"'Cos he wants the ruby," Wiggins explained. "The dewan had the key to the safe. He killed him for the key. Only you got there too quick, afore he could take it off him."

"And now Ravi's got the key," Beaver added.

"Oh, my giddy aunt!" Annie gasped, instantly realizing the danger this meant for Ravi. "Come on – I'll show you where his room is."

She picked up the lamp again and turned back to the door. "Ssh," she whispered as she opened it and peered out into the corridor. "Right. The coast's clear. But you'll have to be quiet. They're still in the drawing room."

In single file, the three Boys followed Annie through the door and tiptoed along the corridor to the landing. A light showed under the door to the drawing room, and they could hear voices in conversation as they crept past it and up the staircase. Annie led them to one of the doors on the next floor up, and knocked quietly on it. There was no response from inside, and she was about to knock again, louder, when Wiggins stopped her.

"No," he said. "Somebody else might hear."

He opened the door and slipped inside. Beaver and Rosie followed, but Annie stayed outside as a lookout in case anyone should come. Following the sound of steady breathing, Wiggins found the bed in the darkened room and gently shook Ravi's shoulder. The young prince stirred, then woke and sat up, alarmed.

"What? Who is it?" he asked nervously. "What do you want?"

"It's all right, Rav. It's me. Wiggins."

Ravi reached out to the bedside table, found a box of matches and lit a candle.

"Wiggins?" he asked sleepily. "What are you doing here? And Beaver. And Rosie."

"We've come to get you out. Afore the captain does you in."

"The captain?"

"Yeah. And if he don't, your uncle will. So hurry up and get dressed."

"I don't understand."

"The captain wants the ruby. He killed the dewan for it, and he'll kill you if he has to."

"Oh, my goodness!" Now wide awake, Ravi leapt from the bed and scrambled into his clothes.

"You got the key?" Wiggins asked as he pulled on his jacket.

Ravi paused to show him the key, hanging round his neck on its cord.

"Here it is," he said. "That badmash shall not have it. Whatever happens, he shall not have the ruby."

"Good lad. You ready? Let's go."

They slipped out of the room and along the landing. Annie led the way, still carrying the lamp, watching out for anyone coming. On the stairs they kept to one side, out of sight of the drawing-room door. But, as Annie was passing it, the door suddenly opened. Wiggins and the Boys flattened themselves against the wall and held their breath. They heard Captain Nicholson's voice.

"Annie," he said sharply. "Where have you been? I've been ringing for you."

"Beg pardon, sir. I was putting that book away in the study, like you told me to," she replied.

"Oh, yes. Very good. Now you can bring some coffee for Prince Sanjay and me."

"Yes, sir. At once, sir."

To the Boys' relief, the captain went back into the room and closed the door. Annie waited for a second, then beckoned to them. One by one, they hurried down the stairs and along the corridor to the study. Wiggins was the last, after holding back to see that all the others got there safely. Once he was inside the room, he closed the door and leant back against it, breathing a great sigh of relief. Beaver and Rosie were both trembling with nerves, but Ravi had a huge grin on his face.

"Jolly well done, you chaps," he said happily. "Isn't this exciting?"

"Never mind that," Wiggins told him. "Let's get out of here. That way."

He pointed to the door in the bookcase, but Ravi held up his hand.

"Wait," he said. "I'm not leaving the ruby for those dacoits."

He produced the key from round his neck, marched over to the picture on the wall and swung it out on its hinges to reveal the safe hidden behind it. Rosie and Annie, who had not seen it before, were amazed.

"Well, I'm blowed," exclaimed Annie. "I never knew about that, neither. And to think, I dust that picture every day!"

"That's real clever," said Rosie. "Any more secrets in here?"

"I wouldn't be surprised," Wiggins said. "But we ain't got time to look. Come on, Ravi, get a move on. We gotta get out of here sharpish."

Ravi unlocked the safe, turned the handle and swung open the heavy door. Carefully, he lifted out the golden casket and placed it on the desk. When he raised the lid to reveal the ruby, glowing on its bed of velvet, everyone fell silent for a moment, gazing at it in wonder.

"Cor," Rosie sighed. "You was right, Wiggins. That's the most beautiful thing I ever did see."

"Quite right, my dear!" The voice came from behind them. It was Captain Nicholson. Spinning round, they saw him standing in the open doorway, smiling in triumph. Behind him, in the corridor, stood Prince Sanjay. They had opened the door silently while the Boys and Annie were looking at the ruby.

"Thank you for saving me the trouble," the captain purred. "I'll take that."

"Oh no you won't!" yelled Annie. She hurled herself across the room and slammed the door in the captain's face. Putting her shoulder to the door and leaning on it with all her weight, she turned her head and shouted to the Boys and Ravi, "Quick! Run for it! I'll hold 'em off long as I can!"

"Good girl!" Wiggins cried. "Come on!"

He grabbed the ruby from the casket, picked up his lantern and headed for the secret tunnel, shepherding the others before him. Once they were through the door, he pulled it shut behind them.

"They must have seen this door," he said, "but it'll take 'em a while to find how to open it. So we got a few minutes' start."

Emerging from the tunnel into the storeroom back at the Bazaar, the Boys slammed the trapdoor shut and hurried into the gallery, heading for the front entrance. But as they approached it they saw two shapes outside, silhouetted against the glass. Two men, wearing turbans and loose, Indian clothes, were trying the door.

"It's the thugs!" Wiggins whispered. "Quick. Hide."

"Where?" asked Beaver.

"Back in the storeroom," said Rosie.

"Right. There's plenty of boxes and things in there."

They moved towards the hidden door, but they had only got as far as the tableau featuring Queen Victoria when they heard a noise from inside the storeroom. It was the sound of the trapdoor being opened. The captain and Uncle Sanjay had found their way through the tunnel!

"Now what?" Beaver asked.

Wiggins thought fast. He bent down and lifted the hooped skirt of Queen Victoria's dress.

"There's room under there for you, Rosie," he said. "'Scuse me, Your Majesty."

Rosie dived under the skirt, and Wiggins dropped it over her. Then he turned to Ravi.

"You stand there and keep still," he said, pointing to a spot beside the waxwork prince in the tableau. "Beav, you and me over here!"

He and Beaver only just managed to plant themselves among the opal diggers in the Australian scene before Captain Nicholson and Uncle Sanjay rushed out of the storeroom and the thugs entered the gallery through the front door.

"Who's there?" the captain demanded.

"It is my men," Uncle Sanjay told him. He called out in Hindi, and the men answered in the same language. "He says they have seen no one leaving this building. They're in here somewhere."

"Then so is the ruby," the captain said. "We'll search the place from top to bottom until we find them."

Uncle Sanjay gave the thugs an order, and they all began hunting through the gallery. The Boys stood still as statues – or as waxworks – hardly breathing and not daring to blink an eye as the four men searched around them. Beaver developed a terrible itch on the end of his nose, but somehow he managed to resist the urge to scratch or even twitch it. Wiggins began to get cramp in one leg, but gritted his teeth and endured the growing pain. At last, after what seemed like hours of agony, they were relieved to hear the captain say that they must have escaped after all.

But then there was a muffled sneeze. The captain and Uncle Sanjay stared at each other and then looked in the direction of the sneeze.

"It was Queen Victoria," Uncle Sanjay said incredulously. "Queen Victoria sneezed!"

"Don't be silly," the captain retorted. "It's a wax dummy."

"All the same…"

And then there was a second sneeze. This time there could be no doubt as to where it came from. The two men circled the wax figure, regarding it curiously. Then the captain gave a snort, bent down and lifted the hem of the skirt. Rosie lay curled round the model's legs on the floor, amid the dust that had got up her nose.

"Well, well," he said, grabbing her arm and hauling her out. "What have we here?"

Rosie glowered at him but said nothing. He shook her, hard, then raised one fist.

"Where are the others?" he snarled. "Tell me – or I'll beat it out of you!"

Seeing Rosie threatened in this way was too much for Beaver.

"Leave her alone," he shouted. "Take your hands off her!"

Abandoning his pose as a waxwork, Beaver leapt out of the Australian scene and charged across at the captain. Wiggins followed suit. And Ravi, standing right under the captain's nose, came to life and threw himself at him. Uncle Sanjay grabbed Ravi and barked a command to his two men, who dashed forward and seized Wiggins and Beaver, holding them in a tight grip.

"You've been very clever," the captain smirked at Wiggins. "But not quite clever enough. Now, hand over the ruby, if you please."

"Can't," Wiggins replied coolly. "I ain't got it."

"What do you mean, you 'ain't' got it?"

"I mean I ain't got it. I've hid it. Somewhere safe."

"Why, you cheeky young pup! I'll teach you…"

"Oh no, you won't. Anything happens to me, and you'll never find it."

"Brave talk, young man. But are you ready to watch your little friend suffer?"

He drew back his hand again, ready to hit Rosie. "Now tell me, or else…"

"WHAT'S GOING ON HERE?" a loud parade-ground voice roared. It was Sarge, who had just entered the gallery. "Stop that at once! Take your hands off that girl!"

"Hah!" the captain sneered. "More brave talk. And from a man who has only one arm!"

"I might have only one arm," Sarge replied, advancing steadily down the gallery, "but you'll find it's a good 'un." He paused to snatch a spear from the hand of a Zulu warrior, and pointed it at the men. "Let 'em go, or I'll run you through."

Then he turned his head briefly to call back towards the entrance, "In here, Captain Watson! This way!" And through the entrance door came Dr Watson, with Queenie, Shiner and Gertie.

"The game's lost, Captain," the doctor said. "Give yourself up like a gentleman."

"Never!" the captain cried. He turned to Uncle Sanjay. "Quick. The tunnel. We can escape that way."

"I think not," said a steely new voice behind him. It was Sherlock Holmes, coming out of the store-room wearing his famous deerstalker hat, followed by a stocky man in a tweed suit and cap.

"Lord Holdhurst!" Captain Nicholson gulped.

"You, sir, are a blackguard. A murdering black-guard," His Lordship replied. He turned to Uncle Sanjay. "And so are you. Mr Holmes and I have just returned from Scotland, where you murdered your poor brother in cold blood."

"No!" said Uncle Sanjay.

"Do not attempt to deny it," Mr Holmes said. "I have proved your guilt quite conclusively. And I have no doubt that you would have disposed of your nephew in the same way, had it not been for my splendid Irregulars. Well done, Wiggins. Well done, my Boys."

Wiggins grinned happily. Outside, the clatter of hooves in the Bazaar announced the arrival of a carriage bringing Inspector Lestrade to arrest the criminals, and a police van to carry them away to jail.

"You're quite safe now, Your Highness," Mr Holmes told Ravi as they watched the villains being marched away. "Your uncle wanted to become the Raja and so gain the riches of Ranjipur, but the only way he could achieve his dastardly aim was to remove your father and yourself."

"We know," Ravi replied. "Wiggins worked that out."

"Did he, indeed? And what about the ruby?"

"The captain wanted that," said Wiggins. "'Cos he needed the money."

"Excellent. But how did you know?"

"His boots," said Shiner. "They needed mending, and he couldn't afford to buy new ones."

"Well, I never," said Lord Holdhurst.

"Excellent!" said Mr Holmes. "I could hardly have done better myself. By the way, where exactly *is* the ruby?"

"Wiggins hid it," said Beaver, "so they couldn't take it off him if they caught us."

"Splendid," said Mr Holmes. "Good thinking. But where?"

"Somewhere they'd never think of looking." Wiggins turned to the tableau and reached out for the jewel on its velvet cushion being presented to Queen Victoria by the waxwork Ravi. He picked it up and held it out on the flat of his hand. It sparkled in the gaslight and glowed with an inner fire.

"Pretty, ain't it?" he asked with a broad grin.

Back in Lord Holdhurst's drawing room, although it was the middle of the night, the Boys were treated to tea and cakes and lemonade while they recounted their story from the beginning. They were served by William the footman and Lily, the other maid, since Lord Holdhurst had insisted that Annie sat with them. She was wearing a bandage around her head instead of her usual lace cap. Mr Holmes and Lord Holdhurst had found her on the floor of the study after being knocked over by Prince Sanjay and Captain Nicholson while she tried to keep them out of the room and the tunnel. She was, said Wiggins, a proper heroine, and His Lordship promised she would be duly rewarded for her bravery.

"What I don't understand," said Lord Holdhurst, "is where this Moriarty fellow fits into all this."

"Quite," said Dr Watson. "I was wondering that myself."

Mr Holmes looked at Wiggins and raised one eyebrow in a question.

"Well," Wiggins began, "the way I see it is this. Captain Nicholson owed a lot of money, and he thought as how if he had the ruby he'd be able to pay off all his debts. But he needed the professor to sell it for him."

"Good," Mr Holmes congratulated him. "As far

as it goes. But I suspect it goes much further. I suspect that Professor Moriarty was behind the whole thing from the very beginning. I suspect that he deliberately drew the captain into debt, perhaps through gambling, so that he could force him to steal the ruby for him, as payment."

"And Prince Sanjay?" Lord Holdhurst asked.

"Ah, that is the truly diabolical cleverness of the plot. No doubt Moriarty knew that the prince was jealous of his brother, and wanted his throne and all the wealth and power that goes with it. I am sure we shall find that it was Moriarty who provided the so-called Thugs, in order to create a diversion."

"Right," said Wiggins. "So everybody would think they'd took the ruby, as well as murdering Ravi and his dad, and all for their goddess, Kali. So it would look like it wasn't nothing to do with Prince Sanjay getting to be the Raja, nor Captain Nicholson paying off Moriarty."

"Exactly," said Mr Holmes. "Well done, Wiggins."

"As you say," said Lord Holdhurst. "Truly dia-bolical. I shall make it my business to have this Moriarty fellow locked up."

"Ah, if only it were that simple," said Mr Holmes.

"It's one thing knowing what he's done, and another thing entirely to prove it. Besides which, you have to catch him first. And, as I know to my cost, he is as elusive as a wisp of smoke."

At that moment there was a tap on the door and Mr Hobson, the butler, entered.

"Beg pardon, My Lord," he said. "But the constable apprehended this young person, loitering outside the front door. He claims to be connected with Mr Sherlock Holmes."

He stepped aside to reveal Sparrow, looking very nervous.

"Sparrow!" cried Queenie. "What you doin' here?"

"Lookin' for you lot," said Sparrow. "I got back from the theatre and you was all gone. And there was no supper."

"I take it he's one of you?" asked Lord Holdhurst. And, when assured by Ravi that Sparrow was indeed one of the Boys and had played his part in solving the mystery, he welcomed him in and signalled to the footman and maid to bring more food.

"What's gonna happen to Ravi now?" Wiggins asked.

"I shall act as his guardian," said Lord Holdhurst, "until he comes of age. And this house will be his home in England for as long as he wants it."

"Will he go back to India?"

"If he wishes it. But first he has an important engagement to fulfil at Windsor Castle."

"To present the ruby to Her Majesty," said Ravi. "And I'd like my friends to be there."

"I'm sure that could be arranged."

"After all," Ravi continued, "without them, we would have no ruby to present."

The footman came back into the room pushing a trolley laden with food, and the Boys tucked into it eagerly. As they were eating, Queenie leant towards Beaver and whispered to him. "What are you going to call this one?" she asked.

Beaver thought for a moment, then mumbled through a mouthful of cake, "What about 'The Case of the Ranjipur Ruby'? Or should I make that 'The Curse of the Ranjipur Ruby'? What d'you think?"

THE BAKER STREET BAZAAR was a real place in nineteenth-century London. It was the original home of Madame Tussaud's waxworks until they moved to their present address, and it was also used as a carriage repository. The Bazaar was built by a mysterious man, who may have been the Duke of Portland using a false name. He really did used to appear in the middle of the Bazaar as though from nowhere, and people believed he had a secret tunnel from his house near by. The duke, in fact, built lots of tunnels on his country estate, as a hobby, so it may have been true.

The Thugs also really existed in India, exactly as described by Dr Watson, worshipping the goddess Kali and murdering thousands of travellers in her name, until they were eliminated by the British in the 1840s. But Madame Dupont, Sarge and all the other characters in this story (apart from Sherlock Holmes, Dr Watson and Inspector Lestrade) were made up by Anthony Read, as was the Indian state of Ranjipur and its fabulous ruby.